Snowflakes and Sapphires

Snowflakes and Sapphires

ISBN: 978-3947985074

To Babette

May God bless and guide you through good and bad times.

1

SOPHIA

I rest my elbows on the edge of the skating rink wall and sigh with content. The view in front of me is just like the movies and postcards I've seen of Central Park in New York City during the holidays. A fresh coating of fluffy snow covers the expansive grass and trees. Skyscrapers peek over the trees to watch the throngs of tourists and residents who wander through the park each day.

I arrived in New York City four days ago. The first thing I did was treat myself to a new haircut. I haven't had a chance to get my hair done in months, due to my tight business travel schedule. It's amazing what a fresh cut and highlights can do for someone. I feel like a new woman.

I glance to the right, and then I see him. "Wait. No!" I stand tall, and my back becomes ramrod straight. "Stop! What are you doing?" I screech, and wave my arms around. "Those are my boots! Someone, stop him. He stole my boots!" I'm a decent skater, but right now, it's a wonder I stay upright. I smack the side of the ice rink several times, trying to catch the attention of anyone on the outside of the rink. Of course, the woolen mittens I'm wearing muffle the sound to the point that they wouldn't hear it even if they were standing next to me. "Please. Stop him!" I continue to yell.

A few people halt and look in the direction I'm pointing, then shrug and go on their merry way. No one runs after him, and it's not like I can run after him with ice skates on, even if I could get off the ice from here. Skaters continue to glide by like this is an everyday occurrence. Maybe it is, since I'm in New York. This is certainly not my hometown in Germany.

Now he's so far away that I can't see where he is anymore. "Shit." I drop my head and shake it.

I was being careful to skate close to where I'd left my boots, and just when I stop to suck in the scenery, some guy snatches them faster than Spiderman could with his webs. He must've been watching for the most opportune time. I have a brain but no common sense sometimes.

My hometown builds an ice rink every year. My sister and I used to go skating as much as we could. We never had to worry about leaving our shoes on the side. It's been years since I've gone ice skating—I'm not home long enough to enjoy anything anymore. But how could I pass up an opportunity to skate at the Wollman Rink in Central Park at Christmas time? I didn't expect this nonsense.

I grip the side of the rink wall with one hand and

kick the ice with the toe pick on my left skate. What do I do now? My eyes dart back and forth, and my heart pounds. This isn't the time to panic. But my shoes are gone! How the hell am I supposed to get back to my apartment? I'm not going to walk home in rented ice skates. I'll look ridiculous and probably be arrested for stealing them too.

A girl slams into the wall near me, and I jolt to the side.

"I heard you yell and saw your arms flailing about." She imitates me, then catches herself before she wipes out on the ice. "Are you okay?"

I chuckle, even though I'm still pissed off. "Maybe I should be asking you. You hit that wall pretty hard."

She removes the fluffy pink earmuffs she's sporting. Then shakes out her long blond hair that has light streaks of pink swirling through it. A knitted pink scarf is wrapped tightly around her neck. It kind of looks like a boa constrictor.

Actually, I might need one of those for the brutal temperatures that are forecast this week.

The girl laughs. "I'm the biggest klutz. Why do you think I wear this bulky winter jacket that covers my butt? It's not just because of the cold. I suck at skating, but it's fun. I come here a lot with my seven-year-old niece. She's better than me. My sister-in-law just picked her up though. I thought I'd stay a little longer. So what happened?"

"Some guy just ran off with my damn boots." I point in the direction he ran. "I bought them before I came to New York. And not one person tried to help me," I say with disgust.

She gapes. "You didn't rent a locker? You can't leave things lying around in New York City. You're basically giving them away."

I look down, suddenly embarrassed. I may be business savvy, but I don't always have street smarts. "I forgot to ask for a locker when I rented my skates, and the line was too long to go back. I saw other people leaving their shoes on the ground. It's Christmas. Isn't it supposed to bring out the best in people?"

"Yeah… it brings out the worst too."

I stretch a foot out in front of me and wiggle the skate. "Now I need to figure out how to get home."

"What's your shoe size?"

"Umm." I'm blank. What is my American size? I've traveled to so many cities, I can't keep my shoe size straight.

Her forehead crinkles. "You don't know your size?"

It hits me. "Seven," I blurt out. "I'm from Germany. The shoe sizes are different."

"Wow, you don't have a foreign accent at all. I would've never guessed. I'd ask you more questions, but my feet are killing me. I need to take these disgusting skates off."

She looks me up and down, then tilts her head. "Are you a tourist?"

"No. I arrived a couple days ago. I'll be working here for six months."

Her eyes squint. "You're here alone?"

I crinkle my nose and pull my head back. "Yes."

"Prison record of any kind?"

I guffaw. "Absolutely not." *What's with the interrogation?*

"Okay." She shrugs. "You seem pretty harmless. I have an extra pair of shoes in my locker. They're size eight, but it's better than your toes falling off before you get home."

I follow her out of the rink. "I can't take your shoes. You don't even know me."

She points to an empty bench. "You can, and you will. I have to go to work in a little while, but we've got enough time to find you a new pair of boots. I'll be right back."

I plop down and almost jump back up. It's like sitting on a glacier with no pants on. Trying to ignore the sting from the cold, I think about her offer. Should I borrow a stranger's shoes? She seems normal and friendly. What if she has a foot fungus? But it's worth the risk and better than frostbite. Right?

Wait. What am I thinking? If I'm going to get a fungus, it'll be from these grotesque blue skates I rented, not from her.

She comes back and sits next to me. "My name is Lacey, by the way."

"I'm Sophia. Nice to meet you." We shake mittens.

"I love that name. Nice to meet you too, Sophia from Germany." She removes her mittens, then pulls a pair of worn Nike sneakers out of a backpack and places them by my feet. "Here you go."

"Are you sure?"

"Yes. I'm glad to help." She pulls on her pink snow boots in a flash. "Let's get out of here. I'm freezing my ass off. It hasn't been this cold in December in years."

We head out to the street and start walking. Within minutes, she stops in front of a fancy store entrance. "This is where I work. I'm sure you can find something in here."

I look up at the sign and get shoved a few times from customers going in and out of the entrance. "Bloomingdale's? You work *here*?"

"Well, I volunteer here for a few hours every Saturday. I wrap gifts for free during the holidays. It's my third year now. I love it." She elbows me, then whispers, "The tips are great too. And Bloomingdale's donates their share to a homeless shelter. Damn, it's hot in here." She shucks off her coat and tosses it over her arm.

I don't know if I've ever met someone so nice and generous. These days, it seems like most people are in on everything for themselves. I know there are good people out there, but I haven't met many lately, especially in the business world.

She leads me to the crowded shoe department and has me try on tons of boots. It's fun, but I only need a replacement. Anyway, thirty minutes later, I'm wearing a new pair and carrying a bag with another in it that I don't need but love.

I'm learning how to treat myself once in a while. I was tempted to buy a sapphire-and-diamond necklace yesterday, until I saw the price. It was so out of my league—but my favorite part was the salesman. He could've sold me a bag of used cat litter just with his kind hazel eyes alone.

He didn't look like a typical salesman for such a high-end jewelry store. More like someone who'd live in a log cabin as a lumberjack. Flannel shirt and boots, a slightly scruffy beard. I don't usually like facial hair, but it fit him. His dark brown hair was a little unruly but sexy in its own way. Then there were his large hands—I couldn't help but wonder how they'd feel against my skin. I even got a glimpse of his perfect ass in his jeans. And when he put his glasses on, I was a goner. Am I weird to think glasses are sexy? Maybe it's my inner nerd speaking.

And he was so attentive! He couldn't be a sleazy salesman even if he tried. His eyes sparkled as much as the jewels under the lights in the store. Butterflies were throwing a New Year's Eve party in my stomach. And then he placed this stunning necklace on me, and his fingers brushed the back of my neck… My heart hammered so hard, I could hardly breathe. Goosebumps tickled my skin and, I swear, my cheeks felt like they were sunburned. But that's where it ended. He got a phone call and never came back. I hung around for a little while, looking at more jewelry with a salesgirl who came out. I kept hoping he'd come back, but he didn't.

Lacey bumps my elbow, and I realize she's still talking. "You have great taste in boots. I should've bought a pair, but I have way too many already."

I give her a quick grin. “I can’t thank you enough for your help today, Lacey. I guess you have to work now, huh? I’ll get out of your way.”

“Oh, nothing to it. ’Tis the season, right? And you’re not in my way. I’ll go downstairs with you. Want to see where the wrapping station is? It’s pretty cool. It’s on the first floor near the side entrance. Not the one we walked in. Come on!” She steps on the escalator first and almost falls forward. She yelps, and I grab hold of her bright pink cashmere sweater to steady her.

“Whoa. That was scary. Thanks for the save. I told you I’m a klutz. My brothers have been making fun of me since birth.”

Should I be wary of this girl? I don’t get a negative vibe from her, and she’s really sweet. She’s a disaster waiting to happen though. It’d be nice to make a friend since I’ll be in New York for a while. I usually don’t spend Christmas alone. My sister said she’d try to come, but she hasn’t been able to arrange it around her work schedule. The novelty of being in New York City will wear off once the holidays are over too, I’m sure.

“Look over there.” Lacey points to the right as we step off the escalator. “That’s where we need to go.”

The crowd in here is vicious. It doesn’t help that I’m carrying around this bulky shopping bag with my boots in it. I feel like a ping-pong ball.

I catch a view of the expansive counter. It’s not only a table with wrapping paper, scissors, and tape. It’s like a winter wonderland. Two exquisitely decorated Christmas trees with white lights and gold-tipped white flowers and balls stand tall and proud on either side of the wide counter. The angels on top look like China dolls. Garlands wrapped in white twinkle lights, strands of golden beads, and crystal snowflakes hang from the ceiling. Against the wall is a massive cabinet with several drawers overflowing with wrapping materials. The sound of Nat King Cole singing Christmas carols lends a perfect finishing touch to the holiday atmosphere.

I would've loved to have had all this for the packages I used to wrap for my parents when they had their bakery back home. We wrapped every order to perfection, and not only for Christmas.

"Wow, this is amazing. Bloomingdale's takes wrapping to a whole new level."

"They sure do. I had to interview for this job, and it's only volunteer. Not just anyone can wrap gifts apparently." She glances at her watch. "Time for my shift. Stay around awhile."

Lacey embraces the other volunteers warmly and chats for a few minutes before they leave. She pulls her hair away from her face, then braids it at the bottom. I stand to the side and remove my coat. She was right—it's like a sauna in here.

Her first wrapped present looks like a piece of art that I'd be afraid to open. A Chinese woman and her little son walk up to the counter. I'm close enough to hear what she says to Lacey. She has a thick accent and doesn't speak English very well. She turns to her whining son and tells him to calm down in Mandarin.

Lacey glances my way with *help* written across her forehead.

I actually can help Lacey. Time to repay her for her generosity.

I step in and ask the woman in Mandarin how she would like her gift wrapped. I translate everything for her and explain to Lacey what she wants. The lady thanks me profusely when she leaves and drops a twenty-dollar bill in the ceramic box that looks like a toy chest.

Lacey's eyes are wide. "Okay, what the hell was that?"

I shrug my shoulders. "I'm fluent in Mandarin."

Some people are born with gifts. Mine is learning and speaking languages. I speak ten of them, fluently. From the moment I started to learn a foreign language in elementary school, it was second nature to me. I was a sponge. Like math equations to a mathematician, languages were my obsession. Teachers were always astounded by how quickly I'd pick up the structure, grammar, and pronunciation. They called me a prodigy. I enjoyed learning them too, so I knew early on that my future would revolve around languages. The chance to utilize my talent in the melting pot of New York City is a dream come true. It's music to my ears when I hear different foreign tongues circulating through the air like a gentle breeze. I haven't been here in a couple of years.

"That was so cool. I wish you worked here with me. New York is bustling with tourists from all around the world during the holiday season. That wasn't the first time I couldn't understand a customer."

"Well, I overheard that the other volunteer isn't coming. I don't have any plans. I can stay and help. If you think my first present isn't up to Bloomingdale's quality, you can fire me," I joke.

Her smile widens. "You have a deal. At this point, I wouldn't care as long as you can translate for me, regardless of what my boss might say. I haven't seen her yet today, so it doesn't even matter."

I help the next customer that comes to us. This is the most fun I've had in a long time. Now it feels even more like Christmas. I'm amazed at the huge variety of paper, ribbons, beads, gems, tiny jingle bells, dried flowers, silver or gold pinecones—whatever you want to decorate your package, they have it.

Lacey pats me on the shoulder. "You speak different languages and wrap like a professional. You're hired. Let's get busy."

We work together steadily for the next few hours. My feet hurt from standing in my new boots. Now I know why Lacey put her sneakers on. I wipe perspiration off my forehead with the back of my arm. Where is a bottle of water when I need it? Someone should prop open an entrance door.

An older man, impeccably dressed, comes to the counter. He asks if I speak Italian. Yes, I do. He hands me a paperweight in the shape of a whale spouting water out its hole. He explains to me that his grandson is obsessed with whales. It's hideous, but I'm just the wrapper.

I inspect a couple of nearby boxes to see if any would fit. None of them do. I step away from the table.

"Hey, Drew," Lacey calls to someone nearby just as I find the perfect box. "Why are you standing there with that goofy grin on your face? Come meet my new friend, Sophia."

I look up to see who she's talking to. I do a double take. *No. It can't be!* The box slips from my fingers and topples to the floor. He quickly comes to my rescue, picks up the box, and hands it to me.

"Hi, Sophia," he says softly. "We meet again."

The corners of my mouth tug higher and higher. I have never been so happy to see someone I hardly know. This can't be a coincidence.

2

DREW

This damn lobster clasp is a pain in the ass on this delicate bracelet. I need my flat-nosed pliers, and of course, they're nowhere to be found. My tools always seem to disappear. I walk out front to search for them and see the store is empty. That's strange because we're usually busy at this time of day. Lily stepped to the back to put the glass cleaner away, and I know the other salesclerk called out sick. But where's the new security guard, Anthony? Someone should always be in the front. I'll have to stay up here now, till someone else comes out.

The front door opens, and a strong gust of wind blows in. With it, just like in a movie, comes a cloud of powdered snow and a woman dressed in winter white, looking as if she were an angel. Snowflakes reflect off her shiny golden-brown hair like diamonds. Her cheeks are flushed from the frigid air outside. Her shiny full lips invite me to kiss them.

She shakes out her tangled hair and combs her

fingers through it. “Wow, that storm came out of nowhere,” she says out loud. I’m not sure if she’s noticed me standing here.

I trip over my feet. “Hi. Are you all right? I just came out front and saw the heavy snow coming down. I thought it was supposed to be sunny this afternoon.”

She turns toward me, and I drown in her cornflower-blue eyes. Her gaze traces my face, then the most beautiful smile I’ve ever seen transforms her features. A few leftover snowflakes melt slowly on strands of her hair and her cheek. An image of snowflakes and sapphires flashes before my eyes. I’m tempted to run to my office to grab a piece of paper and a pencil. This is the idea I’ve been waiting for.

“I’m good but a little wet. Do you have a tissue or paper towel I can use to dry my face?”

“Sure. Would you like something hot to drink? A cappuccino, maybe a hot chocolate?”

“I’m dying for a cappuccino. Thank you. I just finished a meeting and was on my way to a café. Then the sky opened.” She taps the snow off her leopard-patterned high heels. “Oh, and look at the snow I tracked in. I’m so sorry.”

“It doesn’t matter. Snow melts. Please relax and look around. I’ll be back in a moment with your coffee and a towel.” I don’t want to leave her, but I force myself to walk, not run, to the kitchen. Lily comes out of the storage room.

“Sorry. I heard the bell. Is someone waiting?”

“Yes, but I’ll take care of her.” I place the cup under the spout and press the cappuccino button more times than necessary. The grinding of coffee beans echoes off the walls through the little kitchen. The smell of the beans flirts with my senses.

"*Her*? Interesting. Why?" Before I can answer, she peeks around the corner.

Her eyes twinkle with mischief when she returns. "I see. She's cute. A little wet but cute."

She's a lot more than cute.

"Go for it. I'll come out if another customer comes in, but otherwise I'll stay back here. When Anthony gets back from his break, I'll keep him in the back too."

Thankfully, the noise from the milk frothing muted our conversation. I hope, anyway.

I huff. "It's not like that."

"Yeah, right. When's the last time you worked the counter?" She puts her hand to her ear. "What? I didn't get that. Oh right, never. You're a mess though. Fix your hair first and tuck in your shirt. Oh, and wear your glasses…as long as they're clean. Women love the nerdy look."

"Whatever." Lacey's told me this before too, but I don't have time for women. But maybe for this one, I do.

I walk away, knowing Lily's right. I only go out there if someone orders a custom design, needs a repair, or has a specific question. I'm wearing jeans, a red flannel shirt, and work boots. A big no-no when working out front. But today is different. Something shifted in me when she walked through the door. Her smile alone would be worth waking up for every morning.

Did I just say that? I run my hand through my hair, tuck in my shirt, and place my glasses in my shirt pocket. Shaking my head, I fetch the cup from the machine and place it on a matching saucer. Lily offers me a prepared silver tray with a tiny bowl of sugar and a spoon. I add the cappuccino to it and carry it out to the front.

The woman is bent over, looking in one of the display cases. I approach her carefully, doing my best not to spill anything. Her coat, scarf, and purse hang over her left arm. She's pulled her hair into a loose bun, exposing the perfect curve of her neck. I try to focus on that instead of the view of her perky breasts that her shirt is flashing me. I need to control my thoughts.

She seems fascinated by one of the pieces. Her hands rest on the glass. Long, slender fingers. No wedding ring. Why am I imagining a diamond ring on her finger? Made by me!

I put the tray on the counter. "Here's your coffee. Oh, I'm sorry. I forgot a towel. I'll go back and—"

"No. Don't worry about it. I'm dry enough now. It's pretty warm in here." She sprinkles the foam with sugar, then takes a careful sip. She closes her eyes in delight. "Delicious."

"Is it warm enough?" I ask.

"Oh yes," she says. "This is perfect. More than perfect, really." Her voice trails off as she looks into my eyes. "Thank you." She places the cup back on the saucer.

"My pleasure. See anything you like?" I do, and for once it isn't jewelry.

She wipes the froth off her upper lip with her finger, then licks it clean. A spark of electricity travels directly to below my belt. I clench my jaw. *Get a grip.*

"I was admiring one of the sapphire and diamond necklaces."

"Which one do you like?"

"Umm." She taps on the glass. "The pendant with the round sapphire in the middle surrounded by small diamonds. Not the one with the gold chain. The one next to it."

"Great choice. One of my favorites. Simple, yet very beautiful." Little does she know, I'm talking about her.

She's beautiful, not simple. She's wearing minimal makeup on her sweet, heart-shaped face. Her deep blue eyes add enough color to her features that she doesn't need enhancement. Her form-fitting shirt is tucked into her cream-colored dress pants, showing off her perfect, hourglass figure. I would be better at describing her if she were a precious gemstone.

I carefully remove the necklace from the case and place it on a black velvet mat.

"Sapphires are my favorite. I've always wanted a necklace like this, but I don't wear a lot of jewelry other than pearls." She traces it carefully with her finger. "Is it silver or white gold?"

"It's eighteen-karat white gold. The sapphire is a

rich blue surrounded by micro pavé diamonds. Would you like to try it on, Ms.—?"

"Sophia. Sophia Krose."

"Want to try it on, Ms. Krose?"

With her hair up and the low-cut black shirt she's wearing, her slender neck and enticing collarbone are exposed to me. Two of the sexiest parts of a woman's body, at least on her.

Her face lights up, and she murmurs, "If it's okay. This is kind of fun."

"Sure. You're my only customer right now."

"I didn't expect to do this. The snow came down so fast, I just wanted to be inside somewhere. Your store practically yanked me in off the street. And then when I saw the name—Devlin Designs. Someone was just mentioning it to me this morning, gushing over how beautiful the jewelry is here. Weird, huh?"

I want to pat myself on the back from the compliment. "We love to hear that. I'll have to thank the weatherman for the snow. I'm glad it led you here." I walk around the case. "Let me take your things."

"Sure. Thanks."

I carefully lay her coat and scarf over the counter and rest her purse on top of them. When I move closer to her, she straightens her back and stands tall. But she's still about three inches shorter than me, even with heels.

Her magnetic gaze connects with mine, and I swear I see a halo over her head. *Great. I'm seeing things now*. I pull the glasses from my pocket and slide them on.

I've been working nonstop for the past few weeks on an important business deal—one where I have to come up with a new collection, and the clock is ticking. My creativity's been on vacation, but I have a feeling it's coming back. I can't stop looking at her.

Her hand goes to her hair and ruffles it. "Do I have something in my hair? Maybe from the wind? It's still a little wet from the snow."

"No, you're perfect." I quickly look away.

"Great glasses, by the way."

I swear I hear Lily chuckle in the back. "Thanks."

The necklace hangs from my fingers, and I point to the clasp. "This is a barrel clasp; it can be tricky. Let me show you how to open it." I unscrew one side from the other.

"Oh yes, I've seen those before."

"Good. Shall I clasp it for you?" *Shall?*

"Sure. But be careful," she jokes. "I'm known to be ticklish."

I chuckle along with her. Laughing feels foreign. I hadn't realized I missed it. "Note taken. Turn around and let's see how this necklace looks on you."

As she rotates, the scent of her floral perfume or shampoo permeates the air around me, and I'm suddenly lightheaded. I take a deep breath and lift my arms over her head and to the front to place the chain around her bare neck. My hands shake while trying to screw the two cylindrical pieces together, and I accidentally touch her skin. It's just as soft as I imagined it would be. I suddenly imagine her lying naked on my bed, wearing only this necklace. I shake my head.

Where am I? In the movie *Titanic*? If I am, I hope I don't freeze to death.

Her breathing quickens as rapidly as my heartbeat does. Goosebumps form on her skin. She fidgets with one of her pearl earrings, and I wonder—does she feel it too?

Finally, I've got the chain fastened. I drop my rubbery arms. "There you go. Let's see."

She spins slowly, then covers her hand over the necklace. Why do women do that when they try on necklaces? She lowers it as if she read my mind.

I try to focus on the necklace but can't help noticing how it rests perfectly above her cleavage. Why am I reacting this way? Plenty of women come into this store, but I've never been so drawn to someone like I am to her. *Because I haven't been with a woman for ages, let alone had a date.*

I clear my throat. "It's as if it were made for you, Ms. Krose. Perfect length; it rests nicely on your collarbone. Of course, if the chain is too long for you, we can shorten it. The sapphire matches your beautiful blue eyes." I motion for her to look in the full-length mirror that hangs on a nearby column.

She gasps once she catches sight of herself. "Wow. It's even more beautiful and delicate on." She twists left and then right. "Look how it sparkles in the light. I think I'm in love."

Me too.

I'm about to tell her the necklace is one of my custom designs, but my cell phone rings in my pocket. "Sorry. One second."

She nods at my reflection in the mirror. I love it when my designs make my customers happy.

I stare at my phone. It's my brother. I'm really not in the mood to talk to him right now, but I've ignored most of his calls today.

"Hey. What's up?"

"Why haven't you called me back? Alfred Waldecker from Juwelier Belser is losing his patience. He's coming to New York with his wife the weekend before Christmas and wants to have dinner. We *need* that new collection!"

"Hold on," I say firmly, then cover my phone.

"Ms. Krose, I'm sorry, but I need to take this call. I'll be back in a moment."

Her smile fades, and I don't like that it's my fault.

Lily comes out from the back as if on cue. "Lily, can you help our customer please?" I lean in toward her. "Stall her. Persuade her to try on other jewelry. I'll be right back."

She grins. "I'm on it, Drew."

Once I'm finished with my brother, I walk back out, but Sophia's gone. Anthony is standing at the door, and Lily is helping another customer. Sunlight streams through the windows as if Sophia and the snow were never here.

3

DREW

"What's up with you?" Lacey asks. "You're being weird. Well, you always are, but this is weird even for you." She waves her hand in front of my face, but I can't break my stare. "I haven't seen you smile like this in a long time."

Sophia is here. With my sister. Wrapping presents. Looking even more beautiful with her disheveled hair sticking out of a ponytail, a piece of tape hanging from her cheek, and a large silver bow stuck to her shoulder. She must love to wear low-cut shirts.

"Dude! What are you doing here?"

"Oh, I think—this is so strange. I think I know your friend. Is her name Sophia?"

"Yes. How?"

How could I have run into her again? Is this a sign? But I don't believe in signs, or at least I don't think I do. I needed inspiration, and she gave it to me. After she left, ideas of different jewelry pieces were practically creating themselves. I sat behind my computer at the office until three in the morning, creating new models with my software and best friend, AutoCAD. I think my brother will be elated.

Sophia looks over and does a double take, then fumbles with the box she's holding. She tries to catch it, but it falls to the ground and tumbles in my direction. I walk over, pick it up, and hand it to her.

"Hi, Sophia." Her name slips off my tongue like warm honey. "We meet again."

Her smile grows from ear to ear. The man she was helping clears his throat.

She raises her hand. "Don't leave like you did yesterday. I'll be finished in a minute. Don't go."

"You left me yesterday too," I joke. "But I promise I won't do it again. I'll wait next to the Christmas tree."

Lacey follows me and yanks on my shirt. "OMG! That was so damn cute. Did you see how she smiled at you? I'd ask for the whole story on how you met her, but she's almost done. Short story. Spill it."

"She came into the store yesterday. I helped her, but Christian called. She left before I could say goodbye. That's all. Except I can't believe she's here—and you know her too!"

She crosses her arms and rolls her eyes. "Boring! There has to be more to it. She's still smiling, even while she's wrapping that stupid whale."

"Sorry. I'm a guy, so you got the guy's version."

She sticks her tongue out at me like she did when she was little. Some things never change.

"Since when do you work with her?" I look out

toward the store, trying not to be too obvious that we're still talking about Sophia.

"I met her at the Wollman Rink today. Some guy took off with her boots. One thing led to the other, and now she's here volunteering."

Sophia acts like we're not there. We observe her as she wraps the gift and speaks to the customer in a different language.

Lacey continues with a low voice. "Get this—she speaks at least ten languages."

"*Ten*?" My voice squeaks like it did when I was going through puberty.

She slaps my arm. "*Shh.*"

"That's impressive."

"She also has an MBA in something international. Sounds like she's a genius, and she's only thirty-two. She'll be in New York for six months. I wasn't able to get much more out of her because we've been so busy."

Beauty and brains. A lot of guys would be intimidated, but for me, it makes her even more irresistible.

"So why are you here, anyway? I know it's not for shopping because you hate the crowds this time of year."

"I needed a break, and I knew you were here. When do you get off?"

She glances at her watch. "Fifteen minutes."

"I need your opinion on something. I was up all night working on some new designs."

"Is that why you look like you slept in your clothes

again?" She ruffles my hair. "Please tell me it's the collection for that German jeweler?"

I nod while still observing Sophia. Her smile is warm and inviting. I should buy something just so I could watch her wrap it.

"That's fantastic. I can't wait to see what you've come up with. Christian will be relieved. Maybe he can stop being such a jerk. Jocelyn says he's being difficult and more of a workaholic than ever. He's worried that you'll lose this deal. I don't know how she puts up with his shit. All he cares about is his investments."

Devlin Designs has become quite popular in the last couple of years. Customers like my work because I take my time to come up with unusual pieces and use high-quality stones. I don't necessarily make each piece one of a kind, but I don't make many of the same.

Christian wants to expand and sell some of my collections to other major stores. We have been approached by a German jeweler who has a great reputation in Munich. The owner has asked me to create a new collection to put in his store. This will be the first time my jewelry is sold outside the United States.

The problem is, I've been blank for weeks. I haven't been able to come up with anything I was excited about. Until Sophia appeared.

"I'm telling you—it's weird, but—as soon as she walked through the door yesterday, ideas came out of nowhere. I couldn't stop working last night because I was afraid they'd disappear as fast as they came. I think this is the best stuff I've ever made. But, since the jewelry is for women and you're one of my biggest fans, I need your opinion before I tell Christian I have something. So zip your lip until I say so. Not even to Jocelyn. Got it?"

"Yeah, of course." She crosses her heart.

I glance at Sophia, then nudge Lacey with my elbow. "She's finished and she's waving us over."

She elbows me back. "Let's go talk to her then. It's obvious that you both want it. Look at the big grin on her face. And you should see yours."

We move away from the crowd to behind the counter. "Sophia," Lacey says, "it seems that you've met my brother, Drew, already. It's kind of crazy."

Her eyebrows rise. "He's your brother? Yes, we've met, but I never got his name. He disappeared and didn't say goodbye."

"Doesn't Drew make beautiful jewelry? I could sit in the store all day and try on everything."

She leans on the counter with her elbows. Her eyes widen. "You're the designer? You're not a salesman?"

"Only for you that day. You came in just at the right time. I couldn't resist."

"Sophia, our shift is done. You can talk to Drew if you want while I wait for the next volunteers."

She pushes off her elbows. "I'd love that. Let me get my stuff first."

I move over to the side, where there's more space

for us to talk. I'm not the most talkative person, but with Sophia, my mouth seems eager to spit out what I'm thinking. She gathers her things and joins me.

"It's nice to see you again, Drew. I can't believe you're Lacey's brother. Maybe it was a blessing that someone stole my shoes today. I don't think I would've met her or have seen you again otherwise."

"I'm sorry about yesterday. My brother called, and he wouldn't stop talking. I told Lily to stall you."

"She tried." Sophia laughs. "She was good at it, too, but I had a lot of things to do. Don't think I wasn't disappointed. But you can say goodbye now if you want. Or should we start over?"

"Well, first, let me get this." I reach over and pull the tape off her cheek. "I think it wanted to go home with you." I wag my finger with the tape hanging off it. Then I fold it up into a little piece and shove it in my pocket.

Her cheeks go pink. "First you see me covered in snow and now tape."

"And one more thing. You have a bow on your shoulder."

Her eyes widen. "Oh my gosh." She yanks it off her shoulder and tosses it in the garbage can by the counter. "Anything else I should know about?"

I shake my head, trying to hold back my laughter.

"Okay. One more chance." She reaches out her hand for me to shake it. I envelop her warm hand in mine and know right then I'm not walking away from her again.

"Hi. I'm Drew Devlin. My brother, Christian, and

I own Devlin Designs. I'm the designer, and Christian's the brains behind the business."

When she pulls her hand away, our hands stick together. "Oh no. I still have glue on my hand from the last package I wrapped. I'm so sorry."

"I'm not. It's not every day that I get stuck to a beautiful woman."

"Oh, you're slick. And you say you're not a salesman. I'm going to have to get the scoop on you from Lacey." She smirks at me. "Anyway, you already know my name. I'm from Germany."

What? How is this possible?

"I'll be living here for six months. It'll be hard to be alone during the holidays, but I can't complain too much—I'm in New York!"

Lacey skips over to us. "Okay, our shift is done. You're awesome, Sophia. Thanks for your help."

"No problem." She turns her gorgeous smile Lacey's way. "I had a great time, but I'm exhausted. I arrived on Tuesday, and I still don't feel like I've adjusted to the time change yet."

"What are you doing tomorrow? Our sister-in-law's annual Christmas cookie bake-off is tomorrow. Want to come? It's a chance for you to meet other people, listen to some cheesy Christmas songs, and gain a million pounds. It'll be a blast."

"That sounds like my kind of party. I'd love to! I can bring some traditional German cookie recipes if you'd like."

"Great idea. I'll tell Jocelyn you're coming. The

more the merrier is what she always says. Let's exchange numbers." Lacey pats down her pockets and looks through her backpack. "Shit, I must've forgotten my phone at home. I can't find it."

"Will you be there too, Drew?" Sophia asks casually.

Lacey guffaws. "Yeah, right. He nev—"

I cut her off. "I need to work, but I'll show up at some point."

Lacey jumps in. "Let me type my number into your phone, Sophia. I'll add Drew's number too. Just in case." She winks at her.

I want to be annoyed, but I'm not. Now we have each other's phone numbers, and Lacey leads us out the door. The polar air is refreshing for a second, until I inhale and almost cough. It burns my lungs.

"Holy shit, it's cold out here," Lacey complains as we turn left to go down the street toward my apartment. "How long until summer?"

Sophia stops and points in the opposite direction. "Hey, I'm this way. I'll say goodbye here. Hopefully, I'll see you tomorrow. Stay warm." She walks backward, not paying attention to the crowd of people bundled up like Eskimos, weaving around us.

Lacey says goodbye and waves quickly, complaining how cold it is again. I don't turn right away and neither does Sophia. She mouths, "Bye," then flashes me a smile that will keep me warm for the rest of the day.

I mouth it back and wave. She strolls away, and I

watch until she disappears into the crowd. If I want to go to Jocelyn's tomorrow, I have a lot of work to do in the next twenty-four hours. I definitely need to take a shower and change my clothes before I see her again. But first, my designs.

~

"Wow! It's absolutely gorgeous," Lacey squeals, and leans closer to the screen. "I can't even! So impressive, brother. It's your best design yet."

Again, I want to pat myself on the back. "Thanks. It's not quite finished yet, but I think so too. I've never been more passionate about a piece. It has to be perfect before I show anyone else. I'll work day and night if I have to." I tell her how Christian and I will have dinner with Alfred in two weeks. "I think I'm going to present it at dinner. To everyone, even Christian."

She shakes her head. "That's dangerous. Good luck—you know what a control freak he is. He won't be okay with that."

"Well, tough shit. I'm his partner; he's going to have to trust me on this one. I hope he's busier with his other companies."

"I don't know where this boldness has come from, but I think it's about time," Lacey says, her hand on her hip. "You need to get more involved instead of sitting in the store office or at home fidgeting with new ideas. You're the reason you have a business. Without your brilliance, there'd be nothing."

She gathers our empty coffee cups and carries them to the kitchen. I trail behind her and toss our crumpled napkins in the trash. The water from the faucet splashes against the dirty dishes in the sink. She adds soap and starts washing them. "You're definitely in a zone," Lacey complains. "This kitchen is a freakin' mess. I noticed how empty the refrigerator was when I got milk for my coffee too. I had to check the expiration date."

I grip the bar I installed at the top of the kitchen doorframe and pull myself up, my legs crossed behind me. This what I do when I'm mentally blocked and need to let my brain wander.

"Don't you find it weird that we both know Sophia and she hasn't even been in New York for a whole week? Think about how many people live in this city. What are the odds?" I say it casually, breathing deeply while I count reps in my head.

"Finally! I was wondering when you were going to bring her up." She grabs a dishtowel and dries the washed cups and plates. "You both seemed pretty charmed with each other. I only pretended to have forgotten my phone. Now you have her number. You can thank me later."

"When she came in the store, I actually flirted with her. You know, I'm the worst lately." I drop down and catch my breath. "For the first time in a while, I had fun and was attracted to a woman. I've been in a rut, but her walking into the store changed everything for me."

"And there she was today. With me. *Hmm.*" She

taps her chin. “Now I get it. She’s the only reason you want to go to the cookie festivities tomorrow. Do you know how happy Jocelyn’ll be if you show up? You’re such a scrooge every year. But I won’t tell her, in case you’re a no show.”

Our parents divorced years ago. They’re both remarried now. We have one stepsister, who’s Lacey’s age, from my dad’s wife. I don’t have too much contact with Becca, but Lacey’s pretty close friends with her.

I’m not a big fan of the holidays anymore. Dad lives in Boston, and Mom’s in Philadelphia. Christmas used to be a special time for us. I always looked forward to it. Now it’s too complicated. Which day do we celebrate Christmas with Dad, and which day do we do it with Mom? It takes the merry out of Merry Christmas.

Christian’s wife, Jocelyn, is a Christmas fanatic. No… she’s a holiday fanatic. My brother needs to buy another house just for all the decorations they own. Their brownstone would be decorated all year long if she had any say in it. She brings our families together during the holidays. Her parents are our surrogate ones. Suddenly I realize how many holidays I’ve missed lately, and that makes me feel like an asshole.

“What time does the party start tomorrow?” I ask, propping myself against the doorframe.

“Two. It’s an open house, so get there when you can. You’d better be there before Sophia goes home though.” She hangs the damp towel over one of the drawer handles, then smacks her hands together.

Shit. When she does sudden, goofy movements like that, she has something up her sleeve. "Why don't *you* text Sophia the time and address for tomorrow? Make the first move. Not that it's really a move, but you know what I mean. You always were a flirt. Take that guy out of the closet and dust him off."

"What are you? A matchmaker?"

"*Pfft.* As if. My love life is virtually nonexistent. Men suck anyway. My advice is probably total shit."

The lack of sleep hits me hard. "I'll send her a message. But don't get your hopes up just yet. Remember, she's only here for six months."

She swats the air. "Don't worry about that now. There's a spark between you two. Don't let it blow out. Besides, it's Christmas. Magical things have been known to happen."

I shake my head and push off the wall. "Okay, Miss Positivity. I'll text her in a little while. I don't mean to kick you out, but if I want to go tomorrow, I'm going to have to work all night. And I need to get some sleep."

"No worries, I'm leaving." She punches me in the gut. "Make sure you arrive showered and smelling good. Trim your beard. Women like scruff, not a face full. I want something baking in the kitchen, and I don't mean cookies. And don't forget to compliment the way she looks or smells."

"That won't be difficult. Both times I've seen her, she's looked perfect. Unfortunately, when she saw me today, I was wearing the same clothes as yesterday, and I hadn't showered."

She wraps her bulky scarf around her neck. "Slept at the store again?"

I bob my head. "What else is new?"

She huffs. "Man, you need a life. Maybe Sophia's the one who'll give it to you."

I stuff my hands in my jeans pockets. "Maybe."

4

SOPHIA

This brownstone is incredible, and I'm only seeing it from the curb. Real evergreen garlands, adorned with pinecones and glittery red bows, curls around the front stair railings. The Christmas tree in the bay window, sparkling with twinkling white lights, looks enormous from this angle.

A blustery wind sneaks up the back of my coat, making my spine stiffen. It doesn't help that I'm nervous as hell. I wonder if Drew is already here. It was a nice surprise to get a text from him about today instead of Lacey. Of course, it was just a basic text—nothing to get excited about.

Get it over with and ring the doorbell. I shuffle the grocery bags to one hand and press the button. The doorbell sounds like jingle bells. I rub my legs together to keep them warm. Through the fogged glass on the front door, I see someone approaching. The door swings open, and Lacey stands there, smiling wide.

She's wearing a beige apron that sports a reindeer with a red pompom nose. The year is embroidered across the top. Her hair is arranged in two French braids with red and green ribbons intertwined. The scent of fresh-baked cookies barges its way out the door and makes my mouth water.

"Eek, you're here. Come in out of the cold. It's like Siberia out there. You can warm up by the fireplace." She grabs one of the grocery bags and steps to the side to let me in. "Welcome to the party."

As soon as the door closes, a little girl runs toward Lacey and wraps her arms around her side. "Coral, this is my new friend, Sophia. I met her at the skating rink yesterday, right after you left."

"Hi, Sophia," she says sweetly.

"This cutie is my niece. She's shy at first, but I promise she'll warm up to you. Just give her a cookie, and you'll be in like Flynn." Coral runs off before I can say anything.

"Again, thanks for inviting me." She leads me around the corner into an expansive open space. A large, modern country-style kitchen is to the right, and a spacious living room is to the left. The fireplace crackles and burns an orangey glow. Five golden stockings hang from the cream-colored mantle. One has Drew's name on it. A Christmas wreath with golden ribbons hangs over the fireplace.

Some presents are already under the tree, and an electric train weaves through them. A Christmas throw blanket is draped over the back of one of the brown leather couches. Candles are lit strategically around the rooms. Just like in a magazine.

Several people, mostly women, stop what they're doing and wait for an introduction. I'm used to being in front of strangers, but I'm not usually in the spotlight like this.

"Everyone, this is Sophia. Sophia, this is everybody," Lacey announces. "I've told them a little bit about you."

"Hi. Thank you for the invitation. I hope I'm not intruding."

A tall, slender woman with perfect golden hair rushes up to me. She's dressed casually in jeans and a cherry-red shirt, and she's wearing an apron identical to Lacey's. "Let me take your bags. I'm Jocelyn, by the way, Lacey's sister-in-law. You didn't have to bring anything." She places my supplies on the wooden kitchen table that fits the country flair.

"I wasn't sure what you'd have, so I wanted to be sure. That's if it's okay to share my recipes."

"Of course. We love trying new cookies. We're excited to see what a traditional German Christmas one would taste like."

Within the next fifteen minutes, I'm absorbed into the circle. I didn't know what to expect, but they're so warm and welcoming, I feel like I'm part of the family already. I'm glad I have a method to remember people's names. Jocelyn's parents are here, but it doesn't seem like Lacey's parents are. She didn't mention that they were coming either. Drew and Christian aren't here yet.

"Sophia, this is for you." Jocelyn extends her arm. "Everyone gets a matching apron this year."

I take it out of her hand and inspect it. "Thank you so much. It's so cute." Suddenly I'm sucked back into my past when I used to help my parents at their bakery. The aprons didn't have reindeer on them, but the nostalgia tightens my chest and makes me miss my family.

Lacey squeezes my shoulder. "Put on your apron and tell us about your cookies."

I swoop the strap over my head and tie the strings behind my back. "My parents used to have a bakery back home. Our best sellers and favorite cookie recipes are on my tablet. It's in my handbag. Let me get it." Within seconds, I have the first recipe loaded. I turn the tablet around so they can see the picture of the first cookie we'll make.

"Those look delicious. What are they?" Jocelyn squints. "I can't understand anything written underneath it."

"These are called *Zimtsterne*. In English, cinnamon stars. The main ingredients are butter, flour, ground almonds, and cinnamon. The white top is a powdered-sugar glaze. I guarantee you'll love them. Oh! I hope no one has an allergy to nuts." No one speaks up, so I guess that's a no.

"Well, let's get to it. I can't wait to try them. We have a lot of baking to do today," Jocelyn commands. "We need to stay organized but still have fun. Someone play some Christmas carols."

She has the kitchen separated into stations. All the

ingredients anyone could possibly need are on the counter next to the massive, stainless-steel refrigerator. Several baking sheets are stacked up next to the double oven that already has two sheets of cookies baking in it. To the right, a pot rack hangs from the ceiling. Every pot and pan shines like it's been polished. I can't even imagine having a kitchen this huge.

Laughter and flour glide throughout the open space. I feel completely at home here. I've missed family life.

After an hour of preparation and activity, the first batch of Zimtsterne is cooling off on a cookie rack. The interrogation starts. I don't mind, though.

"Sophia," Jocelyn's mother, Judy, says. "Why are you alone in New York at Christmas time? Don't you have family?" Her hands wrap tightly around a red teacup while her glasses fog from the steam. I try not to laugh.

"Mom! Don't be so nosy," Jocelyn warns her, then takes a seat at the table and waits for my response.

I fill my glass with water, getting my hands wet in the process. "It's okay. I don't have anything to hide." I dry my hands and find my own seat at the table. My legs thank me. "It's kind of a long story."

"Start from the beginning," Judy insists. "Lacey told us a little bit about you. Sounds like you speak a lot of languages."

"Yes. I'm a linguist and studied at Oxford in England. Linguists study languages but don't necessarily speak them. I actually do. I travel around the world as an interpreter and translator for Fortune 500 companies. My career didn't start off that way, but my name got around. It helps that I have an MBA in international business too."

I'm not going to throw in there that I graduated early from high school and got a full scholarship at Oxford in their modern languages and linguistic program because of my gift.

"So why are you in New York?"

"I've been asked to be a professor at Cornell for six months. It's a great opportunity, and it keeps me in one place for a while. I need a break from traveling all the time. My mentor from Oxford is a professor there and recommended me. I was asked to come before Christmas to discuss the curriculum… plus, it gives me time to adjust to living here."

Jocelyn sneaks a Zimtstern and nibbles on a point of the star. Her eyes close. When they open, she looks at me and says, "You were right. *Delicious*."

"I would hope so, since my parents were bakers." We all chuckle.

"Isn't it hard to be away from your family at this time of year?" Lacey asks while stealing a cookie too.

"Absolutely, but to be in New York during the holidays—that's a dream come true."

"Are you married? Have any kids?" Judy interrogates some more. I wouldn't be surprised if she had a pad and paper to take notes.

"No. I'm single."

"Funny. So is Drew," Lacey adds with enthusiasm. The women around the table giggle.

"Well, we'll be your surrogate family while you're here," Jocelyn promises, and taps the table. "You won't be alone during the holidays." Everyone cheers and starts chatting among themselves.

"Drew! You're here. What a special surprise this year," Jocelyn gushes and slides her chair away from the table. Everyone else looks at him like they're surprised he's here too. Jocelyn gives him a hug. "When did you arrive? I didn't even hear the door."

"When you started to interrogate poor Sophia. But I'll admit, I was just as curious. So I kept quiet and listened from the hallway."

Oh my. He looks drop-dead gorgeous today. I like his casual style. I'm sick of guys in suits. He's wearing a long-sleeved, olive-green shirt, jeans, and worn brown boots. He's trimmed his beard down to only scruff, revealing the hard line of his jaw. I love it shorter. His hair is more tame this time. No glasses today, but maybe he only wears them when he works.

His gaze rests on me but only for a moment because the guests also get in line to greet him. I stand up and straighten my apron. Should I stand in line too? How should I greet him this time? Shake his hand? Hug him like the others? *I'd like to do a lot more than hug him.* Kiss him on the cheek or pat his perfect ass? Give the peace sign and say I have to go to the bathroom? Or just be a dork and wave?

My thoughts are all over the place. I can greet people in different cultures with confidence, but I don't know how to say hi to someone I'm attracted to, and in front of his family no less. It's been so long since I've been interested in someone or have had any physical contact.

Now I'm the only one who hasn't greeted him. I inch closer to him as he approaches me. My heart is hammering, and I'm aware that everyone is watching us. He's about a foot away from me now and, gosh, does he smell good. A lumberjack in a pine forest. I'm in heaven.

I couldn't hide my smile even if I tried. "Hi, Drew."

"Hi there. You look pretty."

I push my hair away from my face. "That's sweet. Thank you."

"Hey, you two. You're under the mistletoe. You know what that means," Lacey instigates. Jocelyn whistles.

We both chuckle, then look over our heads. Yup, there it is. My cheeks are so hot that we could bake cookies on them if there weren't space in the oven. He peeks at his family and a mischievous smirk grows on his face. He's going to kiss me, and how am I okay with that? The clinks of blinking eyelids surround us… or is it the timer going off?

He takes my chin in his fingers and raises it. His eyes widen, asking me if it's okay. I nod into his hand and lift my chin even higher. His silky lips press lightly against mine and linger there as if savoring the moment. I sure am. I close my eyes, wishing he'd take it further… but he doesn't, and he shouldn't.

He pulls away, licks his lips, and whispers in my

ear. "Cinnamon and sugar. I've wondered what you'd taste like. Tempting."

I just melted like butter. I might be an expert in several languages, but the language of love has never been one of them.

The next hour passes by in a snap. I haven't had a real conversation with Drew because others have been occupying his time. We sneak glances at each other from across the room once in a while. Sometimes he makes funny faces. We both snicker then look away. I feel like a teenager again.

"So where's the next recipe?" Jocelyn says from over my shoulder.

"Did you just hear the radio?" Lacey's loud voice cuts through the chatter. "A snowstorm is headed our way. We might get slammed. It's too early to say though. That's all for now. Carry on."

Now the song "White Christmas" is blasting through the kitchen. Lacey's a riot.

"Where were we?" Jocelyn asks.

I load the recipe on my tablet and show it to her. After we place the ingredients on the counter, I ask, "What do you do for a living? You're so creative with everything you touch. I overheard someone ask you about a clothing line."

"I'm a dress designer. From sundresses all the way up to evening gowns. I love interior design too, but that's only a hobby."

“And I’m her assistant.” Lacey drapes her arms over our shoulders. “I should’ve showed you her line in Bloomingdale’s when we were there. But you were more interested in Drew.” She clicks her tongue. “Maybe next time.” She scoots away before I can respond.

“You must be well known if your line’s in Bloomingdale’s. Did you make these aprons?”

“As a matter of fact, I did.” Her blonde hair pools over her left shoulder. “Every year I make something that everyone can take home after the cookie party’s finished. Last year was a Christmas dishtowel. I always embroider the year on it too.”

Everybody has their own talent.

“Excuse me, ladies.” Drew’s right behind me. “May I interrupt and help?”

“Go for it. I need to check on the cookies in the oven.” Jocelyn gives me a quick grin and moves away.

“Hi again. You’re a popular guy in this house. I’m about to start my next batch of German cookies. You have to get a bit physical with this recipe though. You up for that?” The way his biceps and chest bulge in his shirt proves that it shouldn’t be a problem.

“I had four hours or so of sleep last night. More than most nights. I think I have enough energy. So what’s the name of these cookies? Something I can pronounce?”

“*Vanillekipferl*.”

His eyebrows rise. “Vanilla *what*?” he says, loud enough that several heads turn.

We laugh until our sides hurt when I try to teach

him how to say *Kipferl* and a couple of other funny German words.

I wipe the tears from my eyes. "Okay. Forget it. You make me think I'm a horrible teacher, and that's not good since that's why I'm in New York. Let's get going with these."

He takes a swig from the beer he's holding. "It felt good to laugh like that. It's been a rough couple of months."

I dump the flour and butter in a sparkling silver bowl. "Want to talk about it?"

"Not really. Maybe another time." He puts the bottle down and rubs his hands together. "Tell me what I need to do. I'm the worst baker, by the way. I gave up a long time ago." I hand him the ingredients he needs to pour in.

"It's true. That's why it was such a surprise when he showed up today," Lacey says. Where does she come from all the time? She buzzes around the kitchen like a bee, checking on everybody. I don't think she's even helping with the baking. "But I don't think he came to bake today. He might have come for something German, but it's not the cookies."

Drew sneers at her, then grabs a handful of flour and pretends he's going to throw it at her. She shrieks and runs into the living room.

"She's such a goof."

"I think she's been hitting the wine. Ignore her."

He grabs two empty stools on the other side of the wide island and places one next to me.

"Thank you. My legs are tired." I perch on mine gratefully.

He sits on his, but the stool looks too small for his bulky body. It's sweet and comical to watch.

"Maybe I don't want to ignore her," I say. "Now I'm curious if what she said is true. If you're not here for German cookies, what other German things are you interested in, in this house?" I'm being uncharacteristically bold right now, and it could completely backfire.

He picks up his beer and shows me the label. "This Heineken. Isn't it German?"

I place my hand on my hip. "No, it's from the Netherlands."

He snaps his fingers. "Oh. That's right."

"Is that all? Come on. There must be something else." I smile coyly.

His facial expression softens. "I think you know the answer to that already." With his finger, he motions for me to lean in closer to him. With a hushed voice, he says, "But we can talk later when there aren't people listening."

He turns to the women behind us. They swiftly turn around and pretend they're packaging cookies. I burst out laughing. He points to the screen on my tablet. "Show me what I need to do."

After all the ingredients are in the bowl, I hop off my stool. "This cookie dough has to be kneaded. It could be done with a Kitchen Aid, but I like to do it the old-fashioned way. By hand." I close my smudged tablet and push it to the side. "Want to try?"

"Does this entail me getting stuck to you again?"

The glue yesterday! "Maybe." I bat my eyelashes.

"Then I'm all for it." He gets off the stool and pushes it to the side.

"But only if you do what I tell you to. Does that sound appealing?"

His eyes flash. "More than you know."

My tiny hands lift his large ones and place them in the bowl. "Now we both mix the ingredients together." Usually this is not done with two people, but I can't resist. I want to be stuck to him too.

So here we are in the middle of the kitchen with our hands in the dough together. Everyone's finally busy with their own tasks and not paying us any attention. At least I don't think they are. His warm gaze traces my face, then down my neck, to my chest, then down to our entwined fingers. Tingles run pleasantly down my back, and my mouth goes dry. This is one of the most erotic things I've ever experienced. I catch Lacey watching us. She gives Drew the thumbs up then quickly moves out of view.

Annoyed that we need to stop, I squeeze one of his hands. "We're done." I can hear the disappointment in my own voice. "Now the dough is ready to form into crescent moons."

Coral runs up to us. "Uncle Drew, will you play *Just Dance* with me on PlayStation?" She holds out her folded hands while hopping up and down.

"Sweetie, I'm a horrible dancer. Why don't we play one of your favorite card games? Something your uncle won't embarrass himself with. Or what about Lacey?"

"Lacey's helping Mommy. Pretty please?"

He turns toward me. "Are you okay on your own?"

"Don't worry about me. I'll enjoy watching you both from over here."

"Warning. I cannot dance for sh—" He clamps his mouth shut because of Coral. We both laugh.

"Go have fun."

"Okay kiddo. I have to wash up first though." He lifts his hands to show Coral the gooey dough and then licks one of his fingers. "Oh. That's good."

"Of course it is. Anything tastes good with that much butter and sugar in it."

"Can I have a taste, Sophia?"

Drew reaches over and smears a fingerful of dough on her nose. She squeals and wipes it off. I scoop out a tiny spoonful of dough and hand it to her.

"Yummy," she gushes, then walks back to the living room while licking the spoon like a lollipop.

Before Drew walks away, he leans in close and says, "You taste better." His scruff tickles my ear, and every cell in my body awakens. "Do you have plans tonight?"

"I'm not sure. It all depends." I look around. No one is paying attention to us.

"On what?"

I angle my face closer to his. Our lips are dangerously close. "You."

"Just wait for my cue." He licks another finger and

grins like a child.

"Uncle Drew, I'm ready," Coral hollers for him with her sweet girlie voice.

"Go wash up. She's waiting." Once he's away from me, my brain swirls. What's going on with us? He's here only because of me? I taste better? I never flirt like this, but he brings it out of me. He's sweet and sexy at the same time but I don't think he's a player.

A cookie tray smashing on the floor startles me out of my stupor. "It wasn't me," Lacey claims to everyone, her hands in the air. "I'm on the other side of the room."

Christian joined the party a little while ago. He's handsome like Drew, but he has a cockiness to him that Drew doesn't. He's wearing a long-sleeved white polo shirt, perfectly pressed black trousers, and shiny black loafers. Not appropriate for baking. When Jocelyn introduced him, I didn't get a warm vibe from him like I did from Drew when I first met him. He hardly acknowledged me and continued typing on his phone. He's the typical guy I avoid. You wouldn't catch me kissing him under the mistletoe.

"Drew, I have an idea," Christian calls. "Can you come into the kitchen for a minute, please?"

Drew mumbles something to Coral and kisses her on the forehead. She nods and takes the PlayStation remote from him. He just branded his name on my heart. He's so sweet with her.

Once he's in the kitchen, he pulls a chair out from under the table across from Christian, spins it around, and sits down. He rests his forearms on the back of the chair. "What's up?"

Jocelyn and Lacey join them at the table. I remain at the kitchen island, pretending to mind my own business. Judy keeps asking me questions about my job and also throws it in again that Drew is single and needs a good woman.

"You know how we're supposed to have dinner with Alfred Waldecker when he arrives in two weeks?" Christian says. Drew nods.

"Instead of meeting at a restaurant, Jocelyn suggested we have an intimate dinner here."

She leans across the table with enthusiasm. "I'd love to cook for them. It's more personable that way. You know I love to entertain." Her eagerness lessens. "Of course, if you'd prefer to have it catered or go to a restaurant, that's not a problem."

"I can help, too, if you want," Lacey offers. "I can be the server. Keep the alcohol flowing and what not."

Christian straightens his back and says to Drew, "We'll handle the dinner—all you have to do is present the new collection. The one I hope to see sooner rather than later." His firm tone implies something.

Drew stands up. "Sounds good to me. You know I'm easy. Believe me, you'll be happy with what I've come up with." He sounds confident.

"That's what I like to hear." Christian's demeanor changes to something more cheerful, but he still seems too serious. Too businesslike. His underwear must be too tight.

Jocelyn and Lacey babble with excitement. I hate it that I feel left out of the loop. It makes me wonder what I'm doing here. I'm out of my element.

"You'll have to wear a suit," Christian adds with a chuckle.

Drew's eyes close, but he doesn't respond. He turns and strides back to Coral to finish their game. I get back to rolling the final cookies in powdered sugar.

~

In search of a quiet corner to respond to a text my sister sent me a while ago, I overhear Drew having a heated discussion with Christian in the corner of the living room. I know I shouldn't eavesdrop, but I can't help it. I hang out in the hallway next to a table, pretending to type a message.

"Christian, I have everything under control. You're not going to see anything until it's finished. No one is. Now back off. This is a party, not a business meeting." I hear footsteps and then someone says his name in the kitchen.

Through the mirror on the wall, I watch Christian storm into the hallway, pulling his hands through his hair. He's not facing me, so I make a quick getaway before he knows I'm there. I lock myself in the bathroom and lean back against the door. What were they talking about?

I hardly know Christian, but I can't help being protective of Drew.

5

DREW

It's only six but I'm eager to leave. Christian won't stop talking business, and I'd rather spend my time with Sophia. The kitchen is straightened up and the cookies are all packed away.

"Anyone up for pizza tonight? Our favorite place delivers," Jocelyn offers.

I look directly at Sophia, and she's watching me too. She shakes her head so slightly that I almost don't see it.

"Sorry, Jocelyn. I'm going to head out. Thanks for the offer. Anybody want to share a taxi?"

Sophia waits a beat, then stands up. "You know what. I'll share one with you."

"Anybody else?" Silence. Lacey and Jocelyn stand near the kitchen table with huge grins on their faces.

"Oh. Let me get your coats," Jocelyn says. Sophia follows her to the hall closet.

"Hey, you two, don't forget your cookies. No one leaves here empty-handed." Lacey holds out two bags.

I try to take them, but she pulls back. "Behave," she warns. "I want Sophia to come back. She fits in."

"Me too. Now give me the bags, please." She's about to snatch them out of reach again but I'm faster. "Quit it. You're going to crush them."

Sophia comes up to us all bundled up and hands me my coat. "I'm ready when you are." She looks adorable in her beret-style hat with a flower on the side.

"Great hat. You'll need it outside. *Brr*," Lacey says. She should move to Florida or somewhere else warm.

After ten minutes of saying goodbye to everyone, Sophia and I are finally out on the sidewalk. Shivering. The cold air could zap a corpse to life.

She turns toward the house. "Is there a competition between the houses on this street? I can't believe the amount of decorations and lights outside. There's hardly a need for streetlights, the houses are so bright. Jocelyn and Christian's looks the best. I might be biased, but this house is the only one with solid white lights. That's what I like best."

"Me too. It's what we always had when we were little." I blow in my hands, kicking myself for forgetting my gloves at home.

She turns toward me, her teeth chattering. With every exhale, a cloud of vapor releases.

I chuckle. "Sorry. I didn't really think this through. Where do you live? We can hail a taxi at the corner." I guide her down the street with my hand resting lightly on her lower back.

"I'm staying near Rockefeller Center. It's a small furnished one-bedroom apartment. Perfect for me."

I pull my head back. "Near Rockefeller Center. Awesome. How did you land that?"

She lifts her hand. "No idea. All I know is that Cornell set me up with it. I'm pretty spoiled here, and I'm not going to complain."

"There's one." I hold my arm up, and the taxi quickly stops in front of us. We jump in and I close the door.

"Where to?" the taxi driver asks.

I turn to Sophia. "Are you sick of Rockefeller Center yet?"

"No way. I go there every chance I get."

I smack the back of the driver's seat. "Rockefeller Center, please." Our heads snap back when the driver speeds off. He takes a sharp left turn, making Sophia slide to my side.

She pulls the bags of cookies from between us. "Oops. Probably smashed. Sorry about that. He's driving like a maniac. I'll put on my seatbelt." She tries to move back to the other side, but he turns sharply again, landing her almost on my lap this time.

I wrap my arm around her waist to steady her if he does it again. "I'll be your seatbelt."

She twists toward my body and looks up at me under her lashes. "Is there some cosmic force pushing us together?"

"If there is, I don't mind. You're nice and warm."

She melts into my side. "Your family's great.

Lacey's a riot. I love your brother's brownstone. I felt at home today."

I squeeze her side. "I think they want us to get together."

Her hand lands on my knee, and she inches her face closer to mine. "I know. Maybe so do I."

I lean in and our lips are about to connect. I've wanted to do this since I've met her. The kiss under the mistletoe was a tease.

The driver swerves two more times and then stops dead in traffic. We both grab the seat to keep from landing on the floor. The cookies aren't so lucky.

I guess we won't be kissing here. It's okay—I don't want our first real kiss to be in a dirty taxi.

"We aren't moving," the driver announces. "Do you want to get out here? It's only a few blocks away."

"Let's walk it," Sophia says.

"Sure." I hand him some money. "Keep the change."

I swing open the door and take her hand to help her out. Once she's out, she removes her mitten, stuffs it in her coat pocket, and locks her hand with mine again.

I wrap my other hand around ours and kiss hers. "It really is cold tonight. We don't have to go to Rockefeller if you'd rather skip it."

"No way. I'm sure you'll keep me warm." She drags me with her. "Let's go. Even if we only look at the tree for five seconds, I'll be happy."

We walk swiftly through never-ending crowds of people until we arrive at the twelve illuminated angels.

The shimmery tree is in perfect view. Remembering how I thought she looked like an angel the first day we met, it's pretty ironic.

"Oh no!" She covers her mouth. "We forgot the cookies in the taxi. I feel so bad. Don't tell anyone."

"Mum's the word."

We stand there in silence and breathe it all in. "I haven't been here in years," I admit. "I usually avoid it because of the crowds. Christmas isn't my favorite time of year."

"That's too bad. I'd come here every night if I could. It's so beautiful. On Christmas Eve, I'm going to come here late when there aren't as many people, just so I can enjoy the view when it's quieter. There's something magical about the atmosphere here. Like all my dreams can come true."

She's right. I've never stopped and soaked in the settings here. Couples huddle on the benches to battle the cold. A string quartet plays Christmas songs in front of a nearby store, hoping to collect some change in a violin case. Kids stare into toy-store windows, wishing Santa will bring them something special for Christmas.

"I don't have a Christmas tree, and I don't think I will since I'm alone. It's kind of sad," she confesses. "I don't have any decorations either. I guess I should go shopping this week to buy a few festive things to spread around my place."

"I haven't had a tree in years," I say.

I memorize her profile while she chatters happily. Crinkles line the corners of her eyes because of her innocent smile. Her petite nose lifts slightly at the end. Her plump lower lip juts out more than the top, making it all the more enticing to nibble on. Her delicate jawline begs me to spoil it with kisses. I swallow hard and take a deep breath.

"You know what? We should make this our tree." She casts a glance my way. "What's that smile for? I know I'm babbling. I do that when I'm happy."

"You're beautiful. More beautiful than any jewel I've ever seen."

She fiddles with her hat, suddenly bashful. "You're so sweet to me. I'm not used to so many compliments."

I angle her toward me, so we're face to face. "That day when the snow blew you into my store, I knew then that my life would change. We've only known each other for a couple of days, but I can't wait to discover every little thing about you."

Her gaze drifts down. "But I'm only here for six months."

I pull her chin up so she can see the honesty in my eyes. "I know, but it's a chance I'm willing to take."

"Me too."

A snowflake lands on the tip of her nose. I kiss it. Then another on her eyelash. She flutters it away.

"Just like I said. Magical," she murmurs.

"That kiss under the mistletoe wasn't enough," I confess, and decrease the space between us.

Her gaze caresses my lips. "Then kiss me the way you want to. While it's snowing around us. I don't care if anyone's watching this time." Warmth spreads across my chest.

I cup her face in my hands and watch her eyes drift closed and her lips slightly part. My thumb caresses her cheek. I skim my lips against hers once and then twice.

"More," she mumbles. "I need more."

She wraps her arms around my neck and teases me with the warmth of her tongue. I let her in, and her unique taste sizzles through my body like electricity. A moan releases from me. I deepen the kiss, then her tongue dances with mine. She sinks into me, and I become desperate for more. But I know I should stop.

I break away and rest my forehead on hers. "Just like a candy cane on Christmas morning. That was breathtaking, but I had to stop because we're in public… and I want a lot more than a kiss."

"I guess we need to behave then." She pulls my hands and walks backward. "Come with me. There's a small bar near my apartment building. Let's relax and get to know each other."

I stop short. "Is someone curious?"

"You're a bit of a mystery. I want to know everything about you. And maybe sneak some sweet kisses in between."

When she said small bar, she wasn't kidding. Ten or so tiny tables fill the narrow space, but it has its charm. Soft lighting, Christmas lights hanging from the corners of the walls. Classic Christmas music plays in the background. White candles burn softly on each table.

The last free table is in the far back corner. I lead the way, then pull out a high stool for her. As we take off our coats, she pats the stool next to hers, not the one across the table. I like that.

"Let's order a drink first before you interrogate me."

"Are you hungry? Maybe something little, like French fries?" She grins. "I need something salty after all those cookies."

My kind of woman. After a few minutes of waiting, we take our first sips of beer and relax. The waitress puts our order of fries on the table.

Sophia points to the condiment bottles. "Do you like ketchup? Mayo?"

"Ketchup. Squeeze it all over or on the side. I don't care. No mayo, though."

Picking up the bottle, she draws zigzags with the ketchup across the pile of fries. I motion for her to eat first. Then I take some.

"Okay, let's get into this. What would you like to know?"

She turns in her seat so she's facing my side, not the table. I turn to face her too. Her knees fit perfectly between mine.

"First thing. What kind of business deal do you have coming up? The one about dinner at Christian's house. If I'm being too nosey, please tell me." She nibbles on the end of a fry.

"It's no secret. A German jeweler would like to sell a collection of mine in his store in Munich." I snag two fries soaked with ketchup.

She covers her mouth. "Munich? That's crazy! I'm from there. Well, a town south of Munich."

"Really?" I hesitate. "I don't believe it."

She nods her head. "I'm serious. It's true."

"When I heard you were from Germany, I wanted to ask but haven't had the chance."

She squeezes my hand with excitement. "Tell me more. Which jeweler?"

"Juwelier Belser. Have you heard of it?"

"Hell, yes. Very high reputation. I couldn't afford anything there. It's where all the rich and famous shop. Just, wow!"

I can't hide my grin. "Thanks. What a small world. Christian researched the company's history and reputation, and then we took a trip to meet the owner in person. We asked Alfred how he heard of our store, and he told us Claudia Schiffer recommended us. Oh, and one other person I've never heard of before." I snap my fingers a couple of times. "Never mind. I can't remember her name."

Sophia's eyes widen. "No way!"

"I'm serious. I remember the day Claudia came into the store. I wasn't supposed to be there, but an appointment canceled. She stayed for an hour and bought two necklaces, one bracelet, and two rings. I will never forget that day."

"I can imagine. It's so exciting," she exclaims.

"I'm ecstatic about it, but I'm under enormous

pressure to create something new. My mind went blank and my ideas were shit. Then out of nowhere an exciting idea came to life. But maybe it's your smile."

"Oh, really." She rests her hand on my knee and raises an eyebrow like she doesn't believe me. I place my hand over hers.

"What? No one's ever told you, you have a beautiful smile? Every time I see you, that's all you're doing. It's contagious."

She shrugs and leans away. "It does help me with business because I have to meet so many different people. It's exhausting to smile all the time for business purposes. Even if I don't like the person I'm working with, I try to smile or be polite."

The waitress removes my empty beer bottle from the table and asks if we need anything else. We both say no in unison.

"So, ten languages, huh? And you travel around the world, and you have an MBA? Sounds like you're a hot commodity." I wiggle my eyebrows.

She half smiles, then takes a hasty swallow of her beer.

"Hey, what's the matter? Did I say something wrong?"

She shakes her head and looks away.

I rub her knee. "I think you're amazing, Sophia."

"And intimidating," she adds in defeat.

I scoop up her hand in mine and squeeze it gently. "Not at all. It makes you even more attractive. If a man is intimidated by your intelligence, that's his own insecurity."

"I'm smart and I've done a lot with my life already." She shrugs. "Sometimes guys feel threatened or they look at me like I'm a nerd. Some act like they're in competition with me—who's smarter than who? I don't care. I just want to do my job. I don't usually offer information about myself unless someone asks."

"Why did you get an MBA in international business?"

"Since I work with so many companies in different countries, it's important to understand the different cultures on both sides. Especially when transactions are involved. We can use your current opportunity as an example. You need to know the German culture and business to ensure a smooth agreement between the two. And vice versa. I also have to understand what I'm translating or interpreting."

She would probably be helpful with our situation. Maybe she can guide us along to make sure both parties are on the same page. But we have a lawyer for that. It's something to think about later, not tonight.

"Do you like the travel aspect of your job?"

"I do like to travel. In the beginning, it was amazing. I couldn't believe I was so lucky to see all these new cities. But you know what's funny? I hardly got to see any of them. My business meetings lasted a day or two, locked in conference rooms. Then I flew out the next day."

"You couldn't extend your trip for a couple of days?"

"I did a few times, and it was worth it. But traveling all the time—switching time zones, long flights—it wears on you. I've become a professional sleeper on planes. Thankfully I can travel business or first class because I fly so much. As soon as I get on a plane for an international flight, my shoes are off, eye mask's on, earplugs are in, and the light is out. The flight attendants know to leave people like me alone." She chuckles wryly. "I used to laugh at passengers like that, and now I'm one of them."

"Will you get antsy being in one place for six months? Do you ever think of settling down or maybe finding a different job so you don't have to travel so much?" I've never even asked myself before if I wanted to settle down, but it has occurred to me in the last few days. But how can I think about these things when I just met her? My job has kept me occupied. I haven't had anyone I considered special in a long time. I'm surprised I remember how to kiss.

She dips a fry in ketchup and swirls it around. "I don't think I'll get antsy. I've been wanting a change for a while. I want to get away from the suits." She laughs, but the expression on her face is interesting.

"What do you mean? Wearing suits?"

"Actually, that too. But I want to get away from the executive arena. It's dominated by men and their slick suits. Not all of them, but many have common characteristics that turn me off."

Christian is probably one of them, and he's gotten worse lately.

"When I got the offer for this job, it was a blessing in disguise. I hate that I'll be away from my family again, but I need to do what's best for me. My parents urged me to take a break. I love to teach, and I'm going to get that chance. There's always a possibility they'll extend my contract or I'll find another job. But I can't think that far right now. I want to enjoy Christmas before things really kick into gear once the New Year starts." She jiggles my leg. "Enough about me. Why weren't your parents at the party today?"

"They don't live in New York." I spend the next few minutes telling her about the divorce and how it led me to give up on holidays.

"I'm sorry to hear that. Divorce is never easy. Maybe I can change your mind about Christmas?" She leans over and kisses my neck.

"You already have. More than you know." I rub her back. "So ask me something else." I need to change the subject. I don't want to talk about my parents. That puts me in a foul mood.

"Let me think," she says as she taps her chin. "Did you say you went to Munich to meet the jeweler in person? Or will this dinner be the first time?"

A group of people walk in, chatting loudly. One woman complains about how windy it has become and adjusts her hair. A cold breeze whips passed me. Sophia must have felt it too. She shivers, then nudges me to continue.

"Christian, Jocelyn, Lacey, and I did. We went

during Oktoberfest. It was absolutely nuts. We had a table reserved for us in one of the tents. It's scary how much beer they consumed! People were falling off the benches they were dancing on. Then there were the people passed out in the grass or throwing up in a corner. A lot of couples making out. It was a great experience, but I wouldn't need to go again any time soon. Well, with you I would go."

"Since I grew up near Munich, I know it well. I haven't been to Oktoberfest in years."

"Did you wear those traditional dresses?" I can only imagine how sexy she'd look in one of them.

Her eyes sparkle. "You mean a *Dirndl*. The ones where the girl's boobs are practically hanging out. Of course! I'm from Bavaria. My parents insisted I have one since birth. It's tradition. Fortunately, I have the body to fill it out."

You sure do.

"So, will I get a chance to see your new collection? I loved the jewelry in your store. Everything had such intricate detail and elegance. So dainty and feminine."

"Sorry, no one's allowed to see it until it's finished. I want it to be a surprise. And speaking of— " I take a breath. "I hate having to leave you, but I need to go work on it. I pushed it aside this afternoon so I could see you at Jocelyn's, hoping, of course, we'd end up just like this."

She kisses my cheek. "This was a perfect end to a perfect day. I'm glad we had time to spend together. Is it okay to say I like you even more now?"

I kiss her long enough that we are both out of breath when we split apart. "Does that answer your question? We need to stop this though, or I won't be able to leave you. Let me pay, and I'll walk you home."

Her apartment is only half a block away. Another unforgettable kiss lands us against the wall of her building, and I have to force myself to stop. We exchange a final hug, and she steps inside. I hail a taxi and head home. Once I'm in my apartment and have come down from my high, I call Lacey.

"Why are you calling me?" she yells. "Why aren't you with Sophia?"

I hold the phone away from my ear. "Chill out. I was with her until now. I have to work."

She blows a raspberry down the line. "Work, work, work. That's all you ever do."

"Are you done? I have an idea, and I need your help."

6

SOPHIA

My neck cracks as I roll and massage it. I spent four hours in an intensive staff meeting at Cornell today. Most of the faculty I'll be working with were there. As the youngest professor, I find this a little daunting, but I've worked with some of the toughest businessmen in the world. I can handle it. I think.

Lacey should be here any minute. She called this morning to see what I was doing after work. I have no desire to go back outside to battle the dreadful wind again. My bones were screaming to find some place warm when I was out earlier. I wish I had a fireplace. I told her to come over to hang out, and we can order dinner if she wants to stay.

I walk around the apartment and tidy up, but there's not much to do when it's only me. The apartment is minimally furnished with a warm, rustic flare. There's a long, wide window in the living room that lets in tons of sunlight. A large-screen TV hangs on the wall. A tiny, navy-blue sectional with fluffy, cream-colored pillows is the focal point of the living room and kitchen. A large sheepskin rug lies nicely on the wooden floor in front of the coffee table. The kitchen is narrow with an island that doubles as the kitchen table and acts as a divider between the two spaces. A narrow bathroom is to the right of the kitchen and farther back is my cozy bedroom. This place is so much better than a hotel room.

I was tempted to visit Drew at his store after my meeting today, but I didn't want to bother him. After we opened up to each other last night and then that heated goodnight kiss after he walked me home, I don't think he would've minded. But I know he has that deadline, and I'm sure the store is busier than usual for the holidays. I kind of like being a distraction—but I don't want to be a bad one.

My heart has fallen for Drew, and my mind is trying to catch up with that. My body was in flames when he left me last night—just from kissing against a cold wall! It didn't matter what the temperature was. His lips are powerful. I can only imagine what will happen if things progress. It was probably a good thing we had several layers of clothes on and he needed to go to work.

It all seems so surreal. I didn't expect to meet a man, especially not within a few days of being here. I hadn't even thought about it. Everything happened so fast with this job that nothing else seemed to matter. This is a new chapter in my life, but what will happen after the six months are up?

The doorbell chimes twice. The tone makes me feel like I'm in a spa and that lavender is going to spray out of the box on the wall. I push the intercom button.

"Hey, it's Lacey. Hurry up and let me in. I gotta pee."

I giggle and push the buzzer. "Come on up. Third floor, number 305."

Commotion breaks out in the hallway, and then there's a knock on my door. Lacey did say she's clumsy. What has she done now? I hope she didn't pee in her pants.

I swing the door open. "Hey—" My eyes spring open. "What is this?"

"Surprise," Lacey proclaims.

Standing in front of me are Drew and Lacey, carrying bags overflowing with what looks like Christmas ornaments and a small, wrapped-up, real Christmas tree.

I push the door open wider and move out of the way. Both come barreling in and place the bags to the side. Drew closes the door and rests the tree against it. There's already a hint of fresh pine in the air. Speechless, I rush to him and kiss him senseless. I can't express what I'm feeling right now. He doesn't seem to mind because he's kissing me like he hasn't seen me for days. Our lips were made for this.

Lacey clears her throat. "Umm, I'm glad things are going well between you two. But can you come up for a breather? Or would you rather me leave? I don't want to leave, but I will if I need to."

Our lips separate slowly, and I lose myself in his hungry eyes for a moment. Lacey coughs and rustles the shopping bags. Drew and I chuckle. He wraps his arms around my waist, and I rest my cheek on his chest. "Sorry. Can't help it. I'm so overwhelmed."

"Don't I get a hug too? Minus the kiss." Lacey crinkles her nose.

"You sure do." I hold out my arms and wrap her in a big bear hug. "Thank you both so much. This is so touching. No one has ever surprised me like this before."

I take their coats and hang them on the coatrack next to the door. Lacey places the bags on the coffee table, then roams around the apartment.

I point toward the hallway. "The bathroom door is to the right."

"Ha. I was only joking. I didn't need to go. I wanted to get in the building faster." She pokes her head in the bathroom and then quickly into the bedroom. "This place is great. You're so lucky. Some of my friends live in apartments half this size. Well, mine isn't much bigger either. This location is awesome too."

"Thanks. I'm slowly feeling at home, adding little touches to it. I don't want to buy too much because then I'll have to ship everything back to Germany when I go home."

Lacey sits on the couch and digs through the bags. One by one, she places the ornaments on the table.

Drew stands close to me, and his familiar woodsy

scent makes my hormones bubble. Or maybe it's the tree.

"You seemed disappointed last night that you didn't have a Christmas tree, so I couldn't resist surprising you. I enlisted Lacey to help me out."

"He mentioned that you had a small apartment. We didn't get a big tree because we didn't know how much space you'd have. But seeing your place now, this one is perfect. Drew is never excited about Christmas, so this idea is a nice change. It gives me a sliver of hope that he'll stop being Scrooge."

Drew rolls his eyes and props his hands on his hips. "Okay. You can be quiet now."

I chuckle to myself.

She lifts up a box with a tree stand in it. "Now this was the most important item. Can't put up a tree without it."

"Before we do anything, who wants a drink? Glass of wine? I have red or white." My face scrunches. "Sorry, no beer."

Lacey's hand shoots up. "White wine for me. I need to organize the ornaments. Then unwind and test the strands of white lights before we decorate this baby."

Drew takes my hand and pulls me to the kitchen. It isn't far away. When we stop in front of the refrigerator, he takes me in his arms and devours my lips again. Not just a little kiss, either. It's a kiss that I'll feel years from now, one that makes my knees weak. My belly twists with anticipation.

"I can *hear* you," Lacey interrupts. "Put some music on if you're going to make out all night."

He sucks on my lower lip one more time but keeps his arms around me.

I drag my hand through his thick hair. "Are you going to kiss me like that every time I see you?"

"Any chance I can get." He kisses my nose.

I loosen myself from his grip and open a cabinet where the wine glasses are. I take out three. "Wait, do you even want wine?"

"I'll have red."

He lines up the wine glasses on the counter. I take the open white wine bottle out of the fridge and grab a bottle of red from the tiny wine rack in the corner of the room.

"I'm surprised you're here in general. How did you get away from work?"

"Easy. I gave in and hired someone part-time to do the repairs and other things needed. It opens my schedule to finish what I need to do. I'm the boss, so I can take a break when I want. And my break will be spent with you and this Christmas tree."

"Why did you do this for me?"

He picks up the corkscrew that's already on the counter and proceeds to open the red wine while I fill two glasses with white.

"To make you happy. I couldn't resist." My hand spasms from his unexpected comment, almost spilling the wine. How is he single?

After the glasses are filled, I wrap my arms around

his waist. "Happy is an understatement. You better be careful. I might fall for you."

"Would that be so bad?" He leans in and gives me a quick kiss, then pats my butt. "Let's get this tree up."

I carry Lacey's drink to the living room and place it on the tiny table. "I hope you like this wine."

"I'm sure it's perfect." She pats the couch. "Now come. Sit down and check out the decorations we bought. I tried to remember the ones that you pointed out when we were in Bloomingdale's."

I freeze. "You didn't buy these at Bloomingdale's, did you? They must've cost a fortune."

"No. There's a cute store around the corner from where she lives," Drew cuts in. "It wouldn't matter anyway. We got them for you."

He looks around the room, the tree stand in his hand. "Where do you want the tree to go?"

"The only place would be in front of the big window. There's an electrical outlet under it."

Time flies by as we get to know each other. Lacey turns on *A Charlie Brown Christmas* on the TV. I have never seen it before. The wine flows, we devour delivered Indian food, and finish the tree.

Finally, we stand back to admire our work. "I can't believe I have my very own tree. I love it. You guys picked the perfect one."

Lacey wiggles my arm playfully. "Right? It's so cute! Now you have your very own Charlie Brown Christmas tree." She sits back on the couch. Drew and I do the same.

"Hey, can we watch the weather? The snowstorm

they've been predicting is supposed to be worse than they thought. Up to a foot or more of snow. It sucks to live in the city when it snows. Total chaos. Sophia, do yourself a favor and stock up on food and water so you don't have to leave for a couple of days. I'm parking my ass at Christian's so it's not so boring."

I hand her the remote. "Here. You know what to watch better than I do. Turn on whatever you want." She searches through the channels.

"Munich is not far from the Alps. I've lived through many blizzards. I think I can handle it, but I'll stock up just in case."

"There's nowhere to put the snow when the streets are plowed. Cars parked on the streets get buried for days or weeks. It's such a mess."

I carry our empty glasses to the kitchen island. Drew follows, stacking the dirty dishes in the sink and throwing the empty containers in the garbage.

"Thanks," I say, as I bump his hip with mine.

"We made a mess in your apartment. I should at least help clean up."

I kiss him on the cheek, and we walk back to the living room. We get comfortable on the couch again. He puts his arm around me, and I snuggle into him to enjoy the warmth of his body.

"I remember one crazy winter we had back home. We had several snowstorms in one week with negative temperatures that lasted for a month. You couldn't find the curb because there were so many layers of ice and snow. It took months to get some of the cars out because the snow wouldn't melt. The streets are also very narrow, so only one car could drive through at a time. I shiver just thinking about it. It was a horrible winter."

Drew tightens his arm around me. I could do this all day.

"Look at the map on the screen," he says. "Lacey's right to be prepared. I can go with you to buy things other than water and food. Like candles and batteries? You never know with the electricity in the city."

"There's a good store down the street. I'll probably find everything there. Wow. My first snowstorm in New York."

"Well, keep track of the weather. It should hit on Wednesday night, and it looks like it'll last all day Thursday. Don't wait too long. The stores empty out like the world is going to end."

"I'm sick of winter already, and it's not even officially here yet," Lacey grumbles. "One day I'm going to move to an island where there's sun three hundred and sixty-five days a year."

"Then you'll have to deal with hurricanes and sunburn." Drew pokes at her.

She reaches over me and smacks his knee. "Don't ruin the fantasy."

"Stop picking on each other," I pout. "It makes me miss my sister."

Drew removes his arm from around my waist and turns toward me. "What's your sister's name? Do you have any other siblings?"

"It's only Tessa and me. She's twenty-seven."

"Just like me," Lacey says, then gets up to straighten the star on top of the tree.

"And you're thirty-two, right?" he asks.

"How did you know?"

He motions his chin toward Lacey. "She seems to know everything."

"Lots of things but not everything. And Drew is thirty-one. You're dating a younger man." She clicks her tongue. "Ooh, la, la."

I chuckle. "There's a first time for everything." Drew nuzzles my neck, tickling me with his scruff.

"Okay, before you two start kissing again, I need to leave. Jocelyn has a whole list of things for me to do tomorrow. She's cracking the whip, but she's a dream to work with. I'm going to use the bathroom."

As soon as she's gone, Drew stands up. I grab his hand. "You need to leave too?"

"Yes. I'm sorry. I have a delivery coming tomorrow, so I need to be at the store early. I also need to work. I'm close to putting the final touches on the designs, then I can start making the actual pieces. Time's ticking."

I hate that I feel disappointed. I can't expect him to stop working just because of me. He pulls me off the couch and wraps me in his arms. "Don't look sad. I don't want to go either, but you know how important this is."

"I know. I'm sorry. The more I spend time with you, the more I want you around."

"It's the same for me. I think about you all the time." He kisses me gently.

I grab his shirt playfully. "And your sexy lips do not help the situation."

"Sexy, huh? Want some more?"

"Mmm hmm," I purr.

"Stop!" Lacey's back. "Wait until I'm out in the hall. I'm starting to feel uncomfortable… and a little jealous… and like a third wheel." She takes her coat off the rack and pulls a long scarf and hat out of one sleeve. She bundles up and slips her mittens on. "I'll wait for you in the hall, Drew."

I walk over to her and hug her tight. "Thank you so much again. I can't stop saying it. You've been so good to me."

"I want you to stick around. I haven't seen my big brother this happy in a long time. He deserves it." She glances at Drew and grins. "Have I embarrassed you enough tonight? Let's go. See you soon, Sophia. Don't forget about the storm coming. Enjoy your tree and don't forget to water it."

"I thought you wanted to leave," Drew groans.

"I do."

He opens the door. "Then give us a minute alone, please."

"Ahh. New love. I've forgotten what it feels like." She blows me a kiss. "Ciao, bella."

Drew pushes her out the door. As he's closing it, Lacey yells through the crack, "Hey, I can speak Italian!"

I chuckle. "She's hysterical. Is she ever in a bad mood?"

He pulls me to him. "Where were we?"

I tap his lips. "These are supposed to be on here." I tap my lips.

My mouth is covered with his, almost startling me. I reciprocate with demanding lips and hands. His fingers brush through my hair, then travel down my arms and land on my ass. He breaks the kiss. "You make me crazy for you. It's so hard to leave," he murmurs between heavy breaths. "No woman has ever made me feel like this."

"It's been so long since I've wanted to be with a man. I don't remember it ever feeling this good."

Knock, knock.

"Coming," he yells over his shoulder. "What's your schedule like tomorrow? I'll be at the store all day. We close at six, but why don't you stop by after if you have time? I'd like to show you something."

My eyebrows shoot up. "You mean—"

"No, not the new collection. I told you, that's a surprise."

My shoulders droop. "Okay. I'd love to. What woman wouldn't want to hang out in the middle of expensive jewelry?"

When I swing the door open, Lacey falls inward, onto her back. She was sitting against the door. "It's about time. I almost fell asleep." She twists and pulls herself up.

Drew shoves his arms through his coat and wraps his scarf around his neck. "I'll see you tomorrow." He steals one more kiss.

I watch them walk to the elevator. "Bye, guys. Thanks again." They wave and step inside.

I step back and close the door. My eyes sweep over the living room, landing on the Christmas tree. Every day here has been better than the last.

And then I hear my sister's voice in my head. *Slow down, Sophia. You just met this guy.* I know, but I can't help it. I grab a pillow and crash on the couch.

7

DREW

Lacey and I had a serious talk after we left Sophia's. She likes Sophia and wants me to be happy, but she's afraid that we're jumping into a relationship too fast. Of course, I snapped at her—she's been all for us getting together from the beginning, even if it was only five days ago. But we're adults, not teenagers.

It does feel much longer than five days though. Lacey pointed out the timing of our relationship and the pressure of business, but if it weren't for Sophia, I wouldn't have come up with the snowflake and sapphire idea. If it weren't for her, I wouldn't be this happy right now.

So why do I feel so unsettled? I understand what Lacey's saying, and deep down inside, I guess I'm wondering if it's too fast too. But what about love at first sight?

It's almost seven. Sophia texted me this morning that she'd stop by after closing. Today was busier than most, and I haven't had much time to sit down. This has been the most profitable year since we opened five years ago. I never imagined we'd be as successful as we've become. I have to thank Christian for that with his business and marketing experience.

I walk through the store to ensure every jewelry cabinet and case is locked up the way it should be. The glass cases and mirrors have been cleaned properly for the next day. I turn off some of the lights.

There's a knock on the entrance door. My heart slams in my chest. Not because I'm startled but because I know it's her. I turn around and she waves at me through the window. My tight muscles relax just from her beaming smile. I unlock the door quickly.

I reach out my hand to her. "Ms. Krose. Please come in, out of the cold."

"Good evening, Mr. Devlin. Thank you for agreeing to see me after working hours." She's willing to play this little game. "I can only imagine how busy you must be."

I lock the door behind her and latch the keyring to a belt loop on my jeans. "We try to accommodate our favorite customers."

I place my hand at the small of her back. "My office is this way. Follow me."

Once we're in and I close the door, I cage her against it before she can speak.

"Must you look so beautiful, Ms. Krose, every time I see you?" *So much for taking it slow.*

She traces her finger along my jaw. "Mr. Devlin, you know I aim to please."

"May I kiss you?" I brush my knuckles against her soft cheeks. "Or is that being too forward with a customer?"

"Hmm, only if I get a discount on the sapphire necklace I tried on the other day."

"It's yours if you let me kiss your precious lips as long as I wish." I devour her mouth, and she gives back as much as I take.

She nips my lower lip playfully. "You'll never get rid of me if you kiss me like that all the time. With or without the jewels."

"Who said I wanted to get rid of you?" I kiss her along her jawline.

"No one." She giggles. "That tickles."

"We should stop though—there are security cameras in here. The monitors are around the corner of the room."

"Good to know. I'll be careful next time." She winks. "Can I take off my coat now, or am I going to be pinned here for a while?"

"Sorry, I couldn't wait to taste you. I'll behave."

I step back to give her space. She shakes off her coat from her shoulders and hands it to me. I rest it over a chair. Then she pulls her scarf off her neck, letting her hair fall over one shoulder… revealing her neck on the other side.

"Are you trying to kill me?"

"What do you mean?" She lifts the scarf and looks at it. "It's just a scarf."

I approach her, then pull it slowly out of her hand. "Let me warn you about something." Her eyebrows shoot up. "It's nothing to be scared of. My favorite part of a woman's body is the curve of her neck and the collarbone." I trace my finger from her ear all the way down to the middle of her chest, then across her collarbone. She lifts her chin, exposing her neck even more. "It's one of the first things I noticed about you. So if you see me staring at it, you know why."

She nods with hooded eyes.

I could kiss her again, but I don't know if I would stop. And this is my office with cameras. *Wake up!*

She breaks eye contact and crosses her arms. "So, this is your office. Your workroom?"

I toss her scarf on top of her coat and step aside. "Yup. This is my second home. It's a bit messy." She walks around, inspecting the different machines spaced around the room, careful not to touch them, then chuckles when she sees the monitors.

"So how was your day at Cornell?"

She perks up. "Really good. The faculty seems to appreciate my input, even though I'm new. My expertise is making up for my lack of teaching experience, I guess. I felt like a star when I walked out of the building. So, I'm a happy camper."

"Good. I'm happy for you. With all the experience you said you have, they should listen to your suggestions."

"So far so good. Now what did you want to show me?"

I guide her to a chair in front of a microscope.

"Sit here, and I'll be back in a minute. Sorry to say this, but please don't touch anything."

"No problem. Last thing I want to do is break something."

I hurry to another room where the vault is. I unlock it and swing the heavy door open. There are several small plastic bags lined up next to each other on a shelf. I pull out the three I set aside for Sophia's visit, then lock it again.

When I return, she's looking in one of the microscopes with her hands folded in her lap. I hide the bags behind me.

"Are you ready?"

She sits up. "Sure am. Do I need to do something?"

"Move closer to the table and rest one hand with your palm up on the black velvet mat. Then shut your eyes."

She adjusts her seat and opens her hand. "My eyes are closed. I'm ready."

I put two of the bags on another table so they are out of view and unzip the bag in my hand. "Don't move and don't open your eyes until I say."

"Okay."

I carefully pour the contents into her hand.

"Open your eyes but be careful."

She opens them and her chin drops. "Oh my gosh. A sapphire." She rotates her hand slightly. "Look how it sparkles! I'm kind of scared to have something so valuable in my hand."

"Lay it on the mat. Here's a loupe if you want to look at it close up. Want to try?"

"Yes. I'd love to."

I show her how to hold the gem with tweezers and examine it with the loupe. She asks several questions. I love her enthusiasm.

"Okay." I slide another mat next to the one with the sapphire on it. "Let's put this gem safely over here. I've got something else to show you." I transfer the sapphire to it.

"But… you said there are cameras, Mr. Devlin." Her eyes trace the outline of my body, leaving a trail of heat behind. And when our eyes meet, she grins playfully.

I lock my jaw and take a deep breath. We can't be in here for much longer or we'll end up doing something we shouldn't.

"Someone's playful tonight. You're not making it easy for me to be a gentleman right now." I peck her lips.

"Sorry. I'll behave like I'm a student." She sits up straight in the chair, then pushes her hair behind her ears. A corner of her mouth rises.

"So, back to business. This time I'll place the next item on the mat myself, but you have to close your eyes again."

I grab the next plastic bag and open it.

"Ready?" She gives me a thumbs up. I remove the next stone slowly and put it where the sapphire was.

"Open up."

She gasps and pushes away from the table. "A

diamond! A very large diamond. It is a diamond, right?" she babbles. "How many carats is it?"

I laugh and rub her shoulder. "Yes. It was just delivered today. It's a one-point-five carat diamond. It's for an engagement ring."

She rolls the chair back to the table. "It's breathtaking. I'm afraid to touch it."

"Please don't. This one is only for you to look at."

"I can't believe I'm sitting here with a huge diamond in front of me like I found a treasure chest. It's not something a person does every day. Well, other than you."

"What the hell is this?" Christian barks behind us. The door slams against the wall.

We both yelp. Sophia leaps to her feet, shoving the chair back. She ducks behind me, and I put a protective arm in front of her.

He moves closer to the table and I get in his face to block him. "Christian, what the hell is your problem? You scared us to death."

"What is she doing here? And why the hell do you have one of the diamonds out of the vault?" He points to the mats. "And what is that? A sapphire?"

"Give me a break. I was just showing her what I do and teaching her some things. Her name is Sophia, in case you don't remember."

"You hardly know her, and you have her back here, after hours, with gems worth thousands of dollars. They aren't marbles you can play with whenever you want."

"That's enough! Why are you here?"

"First of all, I don't need a reason to be here. This is my company too. Second, I told you I was coming in to look at the merchandise we received today. I'm assuming those are from the shipment."

Shit. I totally forgot.

"Oh, and maybe to ask about the progress you've made with the new collection. You must have a lot of time on your hands if you're here showing off in front of her." He gestures toward Sophia like she's trash.

"Excuse me?" Sophia snaps and moves forward.

I grit my teeth and ball my fists, even as I stretch my arm out to keep her back. "I'm sorry," I tell her. "I think it'd be best for you to go so I can deal with my brother. I'll show you out."

We gather her coat and things and walk to the front of the store. Once we're at the door, I apologize to her. We're both angry and I can tell she's hurt. Our goodbye is rushed as she can't wait to leave. I let her out, then lock up again and stomp back to my office.

"What the hell is wrong with you, Christian? That was completely uncalled for. You have embarrassed Sophia and me. We were doing nothing wrong."

"You've known her for like five minutes, and you're letting her handle our investments. How do you even know you can trust her?" He paces the room. "We're days away from the biggest business deal we've ever had, and you're in here flirting and showing off and God knows what else."

"Take Sophia out of the equation. She has done nothing to you, and I trust her."

"How can you trust someone you hardly know?"

I get up in his face. "Let me tell you this right now, big brother. You watch what you say from here on out. You can't stand that you can't control me. I *told* you, I'll have the collection ready. And it *will* be ready. What I do on my own time is none of your fucking business."

I stride back to the table, place the diamond and sapphire in their corresponding bags, and zip them up. Then I take the other bag and go to the vault. Christian's footsteps pound on the floor behind me.

"Are you sure you put them in the right bags? I want to check them before you put them away."

I roll my eyes as I place the jewels in the vault and set the lock. Then I turn around, consciously reining in my anger. "I control this store and everything that's in it every fucking day. Do not question my abilities or judgment. *Ever*. Do I make myself clear?"

His face reveals no emotion. Just solid stone. He spins on his heel and barges out the door.

This is not how I wanted this evening to end. All I can see is the anger and sadness that was sketched all over Sophia's face.

8

SOPHIA

I've had my phone on mute since I left Drew's store last night. He tried to call once but I didn't answer. Then he texted, asking me to call him. Lacey called too, but I sent her to voicemail. I'm still confused about what happened at the store, and I don't have the energy to talk to them right now. Christian made me feel like I was trying to steal their stuff. What am I supposed to say?

I couldn't sleep most of the night, so I called Tessa. It's nice that she's six hours ahead of the East Coast. She let me spill my guts about my growing feelings toward Drew and the store situation before she offered her advice. She's younger than I am, but has a lot more experience when it comes to dating.

"You did nothing wrong. It sounds like a family issue. Drew knew what he was doing, so if there's anyone to blame, it's him.

I understand Christian's anger to an extent because diamonds and sapphires aren't toys or cheap."

"I get that. But Drew was very professional and careful. Christian thought he was trying to show off. I didn't get that feeling at all. My gut was that he was trying to do something nice for me. Like with the Christmas tree."

"Maybe you're right. But put yourself in Christian's shoes. He doesn't know you. You kind of showed up out of the blue. Now, only a couple days later, you're in the back of the store surrounded by expensive gems." She laughs. "I'm happy you weren't screwing around. Anyway, I probably wouldn't trust the situation either. He also looks at you as a major distraction when he needs Drew to focus on something more important. Just remember, it's business and family. I don't think it's personal. It's between them."

"But what do I do with my feelings for Drew? No one has ever made me feel like I do with him. And no, I don't think it's because it's Christmas and I'm alone. I'm used to being alone. You know that. It would crush me if… if whatever we have… was over just because of this."

"Why don't you keep to yourself for a couple of days? Let it blow over. Focus on your job—that should be your priority anyway. Sorry to say it, Sis, but it shouldn't be Drew."

"I know. That shouldn't be a problem anyway, since we're supposed to be getting a blizzard tomorrow. I'll be stuck in this apartment. I'll have enough work to keep me busy, and thanks to Drew, I have a Christmas tree to enjoy."

When we hung up, I wasn't feeling any better. And now it's several hours later, and I still don't. But it's time to get ready for the blizzard everyone's so worked up about.

The sliding glass door to the grocery store opens. I walk in and stop dead. People are swarming in here. It's like there was a massive sale. Shelves are empty! I walk through the aisles to find signs stating that water and milk are sold out. I do manage to snag the last loaf of bread. There are no candles or batteries either. I found two flashlights in the apartment, but they didn't have batteries. Not exactly helpful. I really have a hard time believing this storm will be so bad that New York City will be at a standstill for days. I can't imagine losing electricity in a modern city like this.

I stock up on anything I can find to munch on for days. Once I'm back at my apartment, I do a search on my phone for another store to see if I can find batteries, water, and candles. The next store is even more crowded, but it does have a little bit of stock left.

"Now the forecast says it will start midday tomorrow and continue into Thursday," comments an older woman to her friend while scrolling through her phone.

"We better not lose power like we did with the last bad storm. I didn't have enough candles. That's why my place is always stocked up with them." She looks at the woman's phone. "Are they still predicting one and a half feet?"

I quickly convert feet into centimeters in my head. We use the metric system in Germany. I realize it is a lot of snow.

"Yes. But hopefully they're wrong and we'll get less. If we're lucky, the snow will melt quickly—temps are supposed to rise a little bit by the weekend. On the other hand, it would be nice to have some snow around Christmas."

I look at my cart and hope I have enough supplies. This storm will force me to stay away from Drew. But I'm not happy about that, and neither is my heart.

~

Okay. I believe the weather forecast now. The snow has been coming down like it did the day I was blown into Drew's store, only it hasn't stopped for hours. It's quite beautiful, watching the snow and wind dance around each other outside my living room window. I'm curled up on my couch with a red fleece blanket I bought at the last minute. Unlit candles are spread around the room in case the power goes out. It would be pretty romantic if I weren't alone and they were actually lit.

I'm supposed to be working from home, but my mind keeps drifting back to Drew. He tried to call me again, but he didn't leave a message. I replay the conversation I had with my sister in my mind. *I should keep to myself.* Well, I've done that for two days, and I'm ready to pull my hair out. How can I possibly miss this man—he's practically a stranger!—as much as I do?

My phone pings. I search for it beneath the blanket. I tap the screen. Lacey.

Lacey: Hey, Sophia. Are you safe at home?

Me: Hi! Yes. No problems here so far.

Lacey: Want some company?

What does she mean? There's a blizzard outside, and she wants to come over? *Buzz, buzz.* No way! She can't be outside my building! I dart to the door and hit the button to let her in.

Me: You're nuts!

Lacey: I know, but you'll love me for it.

I stand still and stare at my phone. *I'll love her for it? What does that mean?* Through my door, I hear noise in the hallway. I swing it open and almost scream because it's not Lacey.

"*Drew?* What the—" I look him up and down. My heartrate kicks up because I'm thrilled that he's here, but he's also covered in snow. "Get in here. You must be freezing. You're crazy, walking around in this storm." I yank his coat sleeve and pull him inside. Two bags hang from his hands.

"Give me the bags and take off your clothes—" I gulp. "Sorry, I meant your coat and hat."

He hasn't said a word, but I heard him chuckle after my slip of the tongue. I snatch the wet bags and place them on the island.

He drops his backpack to the floor, then pulls off his hat. His hair spikes out in all directions. The messy hair makes him sexier than ever. His warm eyes say hello better than the real word.

I saunter up to him and hold out my hand. "Give me your hat, gloves, and scarf. I'll lay them on the radiator." He hands them to me, and I take them over to the heater.

Rustling sounds of him taking off his coat and shoes circulate the room. Just as I lay his hat on the radiator, I feel him behind me.

"Hi, Sophia."

I wipe my wet hands on my sweatpants and turn around. His hair is still a mess, and his sweater is tight enough that I can see the outline of his muscular shoulders and chest. Not good, because my body goes immediately on high alert. I don't think I could resist him even if I try. I want to kiss him, but I stay put.

"Hi there. I can't believe you're here. It's so dangerous outside. Why would you do that?"

"Because I can't stand that we haven't spoken since you left my store. I felt—and still feel—horrible about what happened. Then I thought about how you'd be alone during this storm, so I took the chance that maybe you'd let me in. You can hate Christian, but please don't hate me."

"Lacey was good. It didn't even occur to me that you were at my door. Not to be mean to her, but I'm happier that it's you. A lot happier."

"Does that mean we're okay?"

"Let's not talk about it right now." I step around him. "Are your clothes wet? Do you need a towel?"

He looks down and scans his clothes. "My pants are a little wet at the bottom, but I don't care. They'll dry. I'm fine." Now I'm the one who's scanning his pants from bottom to top. Everything about him right now is causing body parts that I haven't used in a long time to come to life.

"Sophia, be honest with me. Should I leave? I can't explain it, but I feel like something has changed. Like there's a wall between us. Is it because of Christian, or have I done something to push you away?"

My temples pound from frustration and confusion. "You really want to know?" I grumble.

His arms open to the sides. "Yes. Tell me. I didn't walk through a snowstorm just to bring you candles."

"I think about you all the time. More than anyone else. Why is it so easy to be around you? Like we've known each other for years. I crave your delicious lips every time I see you. I'm jealous of the jewelry you touch every day because I want to be the one your hands are on. You have no idea how special you make me feel. With the Christmas tree and then showing me the diamonds and sapphires… You are the most generous person I've ever met, and I haven't even known you a whole week."

He growls. "Why is everyone so fixated on how long we have or haven't known each other. Why is a week so bad?"

I rub my face and pull my hands through my messy hair. "I'm wondering if I'm falling for you for the wrong reasons. But when I think of those reasons, my heart yells at me and tells me to shut up."

"I have to agree with your heart. Being away from you since Monday night has been torture. But I needed time to understand my feelings too."

“But I don’t want us, *this*, to interfere with your work. I couldn’t live with that. Christian is a bit too intense—to say it nicely—but I don’t want to cause tension between you two. Maybe it’d be better if we wait until after your deal to see each other.”

“We’re adults, and I know what’s right for me. And *you* are right for *me*. Do you understand? Let’s get to know each other, but I hope there’ll be a lot of kissing in the process.” His eyes switch from warm to blazing.

I ease toward him. “Only kissing? I don’t know if I can resist you much longer. Maybe I can’t hold back. It’s been a long time since I’ve been with a man.” I laugh, surprised at myself. “One thing I love about us is that I’m bolder than I’ve ever been.”

He lifts his arm and cups the back of my neck, then tugs me forward. “Can I kiss you now, or is there something else we need to talk about?”

I place my finger on his lips. “I’d love for you to kiss me with your enticing lips but—” I break away from him. “If you don’t mind, I’d like to freshen up. I wasn’t expecting a lumberjack this evening. I would’ve worn something sexier than sweatpants and a ratty old sweatshirt.”

9

DREW

I laugh. "A lumberjack?"

"It's what I thought of the first time I saw you. I like it. How can such a big guy work with such delicate things?"

I steal a small taste of her. "I'll show you later. Now stop talking. Go do what you need to do. I'll be waiting. But tell me when you're finished. I have another surprise for you, so don't come out until I say so."

"You spoil me. Don't think I don't love it." She walks backward with my favorite smile on her face, then she disappears behind closed doors.

I already had a plan, hoping that tonight would lead to this perfect moment. The bags I brought are in the kitchen. I scan the room for the perfect placement of the candles I brought. What's even better is that she's already prepared for the electricity to go out too. This makes my job even easier.

She turns on the water in the shower. Oh, how I

wish I were in there with her. But I need to be patient and control myself. There's plenty of time for that. I spend the next few minutes setting up the living room the way I envisioned. Blankets and pillows on the sheepskin rug. Not bad for someone who's never done this before and never wanted to until now.

The view outside is like someone shook a snow globe. The wind rattles the windows, asking to come in. The worst of the storm hasn't even started yet.

My phone vibrates on the coffee table. I glance at it. Lacey.

Lacey: Everything okay?
Me: Yes. Don't bother us for a couple days.
Lacey: State of emergency was declared. You can't leave anyway. Use protection.

Lacey might be a little worried about our relationship, but she's always been supportive of me. We've always had a close relationship and often confide in each other. Christian's the serious one. I shake my head. I don't want to think about him. I turn off my phone. No more interruptions.

Sophia calls me from the bathroom. "I'm finished."

"I'm coming. Don't open the door." I scope out the living room one more time to make sure everything is perfect.

Once I'm satisfied, I take a deep breath, then exhale. "Sophia, when you come out, please keep your eyes shut."

"What do you have up your sleeve now? Okay. Here I come." The door opens slowly, and she steps out, one hand over her eyes.

"Squeeze them shut. No peeking."

When I see her, my stomach jumps with excitement, and my mouth goes dry. Her hair is up, revealing her neck, which is killing me already. She's wearing a short white robe that reveals her long, slender legs.

She sniffs. "Candles. Hmm. You are a man full of surprises. I can't wait to see what you've done this time."

"Let me guide you." I lead her to the little bed I've made. "Stop here and step to the right."

She skims her foot over the surface. "Ooh. What's that? A blanket?"

"So curious. You'll see. Now hold onto me and kneel on the floor."

"Kneel? Oookay." She wiggles then regains her balance once she's on her knees.

"Ready?"

She nods with a giddy smile.

"Open your eyes."

She flutters her eyelashes and covers her mouth. "This is an absolute dream. I don't know what to say. I can't believe you did this."

"They've declared a state of emergency. I guess I have to stay here."

She props her hands on her hips. "I wonder what we can do all night?"

I point at her robe. "You're not cold?"

"A little, but I have a feeling I won't be for long. There are enough candles burning in here to keep me warm—and if they don't, I'm sure you'll help."

The anticipation weighs heavily in the room. We face each other with a few inches between us. Our breathing increases. I close the space between us and cover her mouth with mine. She wraps her arms around my waist and frantically grips the bottom of my shirt, interrupting the kiss. Then she pulls it over my head.

Her heated gaze explores my chest and abs. "I never knew a jeweler could be so trim." She cocks her head. "Or what would Americans say… ripped?" She plants kisses all over my chest and brushes her fingers over the ridges of my abs, continuing lower. I shiver in delight when she whispers, "*Mmm*, I can't wait to see what's down here."

"Did I ever tell you what part of the female body is my favorite?"

"Yes, you did. But I want you to show me. Not tell me," she says playfully.

I rub her arms. "Are you sure you want this? Just say the word."

"I want this, Drew. I want you. Come closer."

I untie her belt and let it hang. The robe parts slightly, teasing me with her warm, bare skin. Her chest rises and falls. I slide both sides open, then skim my fingers over her stomach to her back, then down her backside. "Your skin is like satin." My fingers continue up her sides, then brush over her firm peaks.

She arches her back and the robe falls off her shoulders, revealing her perfect breasts.

She shivers.

"You *are* cold."

"No." She caresses my cheek. "It's being close to you like this. What's going on in my head, heart, and body is nothing I've experienced before. It's almost like I can't breathe because it's so amazing. Is this what it's like to fall for someone?"

I wrap an arm around her lower back and trace along her collarbone with my other hand. "I think so, because I feel it too." My eager lips and tongue explore where my fingers just were and then up the luscious skin of her neck. She arches her head back and teases my chest with her breasts.

"I love the way you taste. The way you smell," I say between painful breaths. "My body aches for you."

"I want your warm hands to touch me everywhere," she says, her gaze full of lust.

"Should I start here?" I murmur against her cheek, slowly massaging one swollen breast. She nods with hooded eyes, then places my free hand on the other and squeezes. Electric bolts of desire shoot through my body.

I claim her lips once more and gently ease her down onto the blanket. I pull back and gaze at her. She's a vision, lying there on her back, displaying her sensuous body for me. Only for me.

She rotates to her side and props her head on her

hand. Her lips curl into a seductive smile. "Why am I the only one naked? I want to see the rest of you." Her hand reaches out to toy with the button of my jeans.

They're off within seconds; her smoldering eyes watch me steadily the entire time. Turning me on even more. I lean over her with one hand at the side of her head.

"You're perfect," she murmurs while her needy hands explore and stroke my heated body.

I trace a line with my finger down her neck, between her heaving breasts, over the rounded curve of her hip, and to the back of the knee.

"I can't take it anymore. Please don't stop," she mumbles as she opens up for me.

"Never."

~

We collapse on the blanket, breathing heavily. I pull her back to my chest and spoon her. "That was incredible." She snuggles up against me, squeezing my arms tight around her. "You okay?"

She giggles. "More than okay. I can't even describe how I feel right now. I need to catch my breath."

I push her hair away and nip her shoulder. She rubs up against me. "Behave. I need a few minutes to recover."

She looks toward the window, then reaches to pull a blanket over us. "It's still snowing. I guess we get to stay right where we are. No one's going to miss us."

"I love the sound of that."

"Wrapped up naked with you on a snowy day? It's the perfect Christmas gift."

We lie there for a few moments, enjoying the utter silence a snowstorm brings.

"I hope we weren't too loud." She chuckles.

"I highly doubt we're the only ones having sex in this building during a blizzard. If we are, I feel bad for the others."

She flips over to face me, then strokes my face with the back of her hand. I wrap my arm around her so we're chest to chest.

"Can I ask you something?"

"Sure," she says with a sleepy whisper.

"Will you be my date at the dinner party next weekend? I'd love for you to be there with me. I can show off my beautiful and smart girlfriend."

She inches away from me. "Are you sure you want that? Christian and I haven't exactly hit it off."

"I'll deal with him. He's not easy for any of us right now. Too much on his plate. You're the only one I want there with me. No one else." I nibble her lips.

"Since I'm from Munich, it might help with the flow of conversation. I could help if any issues arise. Translate if you need it. That's *if* I say yes."

"That would be great. We haven't had any communication issues yet, but you never know. Thank you. Do you mind dressing up? I have to wear a suit. I only wear one when I have to."

"I might be sick of men in suits, but I have a feeling you'll look handsome." She twirls a piece of my hair around her finger. "That's reason enough to say yes."

"Don't torture me. What do you say?" I tickle her side.

"As long as it won't cause a problem with your brother, I'd love to."

"Believe me, by the end of the night, you'll be his favorite person. You're already mine."

"I'm not sure I want to know what that means, but I don't care. I just want to be with you. And I'd love to see Lacey and Jocelyn again."

"Then it's a date."

10

SOPHIA

Once the storm stopped and New York City was back in motion, I called Lacey for help. I have no idea what I should wear for this dinner party. She told me to meet her at Jocelyn's on Sunday. I asked her why there, but she said not to worry about it, just be there.

So here I am, standing in front of Jocelyn's brownstone just like a week ago. It feels like months with everything that's happened since then. Drew didn't leave my apartment until Friday morning when the state of emergency was lifted. His store was closed because of it, so he had nowhere to be except in my warm bed. We didn't complain.

Even after spending so much time with him, I couldn't get enough. I would've had him stay longer. He said the same, but he needed to get to work since he'd missed a full day on the designs. I've been walking on cloud nine ever since. He is the most beautiful, caring soul I've ever met. How could I not fall for him?

"Hi, Sophia," Jocelyn says happily. "Come on in. We're going to have some fun today."

I walk through the door and Lacey comes around the corner from the living room. She gives me a hug. "I've been looking forward to this so much. Let's get started."

"We could've met in the city to go shopping," I say as Lacey removes my coat for me, then pulls my hat off my head. The snap of static follows. I pat my hair down.

"Oh, we're not going to the city. Where we're going is a lot more fun and private." Jocelyn giggles, then winks at Lacey.

"Please take off your shoes."

"But I thought we were leaving. What have you girls got up your sleeves? You make me nervous."

They loop their arms through mine and lead me to the stairs. "No need to be. Let's just say we're going to play—well, no—*you* are going to play dress up."

"Upstairs in your house?" I say with confusion.

With arms still linked in mine, we walk up two sets of stairs. I haven't been in this part of the house. Of course, it's impeccably decorated like the first floor. We stop in front of a white door.

Jocelyn turns to face me, her hand on the doorknob, a silly grin on her face. "Remember when I told you I'm a dress designer?"

"Yes." I think I know where this is going now.

Lacey chimes in. "Well, what we didn't tell you is

that she has a room full of her designs in this house. A mini boutique. Check it out."

Jocelyn pushes the door open gently. I step in and clasp my hands to my chest. This is so much better than a store. The room is set up like an elegant dressing room. It's even decorated for Christmas.

Each wall is lined with racks of dresses and gowns, sorted by the colors of the rainbow. A powder-puff-pink couch sits in the middle of the room on plush ivory carpet, facing an elegant pink-curtained doorway that leads to what I assume is a private changing room. Just outside the room is a three-way floor-length mirror, a small rectangular platform in front of it. A champagne bottle relaxes in a bucket of ice on a low table in front of the couch. Crystal champagne flutes wait patiently to be filled. Large gold and pink Christmas balls that match the decorated tree in front of the window are arranged strategically across the table surface.

"What do you think?" Jocelyn says, twirling with her arms wide open. "It's my favorite room."

"It's like a mini mall inside your house. It's perfect. Do I get to try on these dresses?"

Lacey plops onto the couch. "You not only get to try them on, but if you find one you like, you can borrow it for Saturday."

I cup my hands around the back of my neck. "I don't know. These dresses are so elegant. This is awfully generous but… what if I spill something on it?"

Jocelyn shrugs. "It's called dry-cleaning. Well,

hopefully that'll work. It doesn't matter. I love doing this for people. Especially if someone falls in love with one of the dresses."

I cross my arms, hesitant to touch anything, and stroll around the room. Every type of style hangs from the shiny silver bars. My excitement kicks up a notch.

"You're both wearing dresses like these, right? I don't want to be overdressed."

"Of course. We've already picked ours out, but we'll show you them later. We need to dress to impress," Lacey declares.

"If you put it that way... let's get started," I say.

Jocelyn removes the champagne from the bucket and dries off the bottle. "First, since I'm on my own today, we'll start this ladies' day off with some bubbly. Coral is with my parents until tomorrow. They're taking her to see Santa Claus. Christian's off doing whatever."

I sit next to Lacey on the couch. "You guys are so full of surprises. I don't think I've ever been this spoiled in my life. I wish my sister was here to join in the fun. I feel like I'm looking for a wedding dress."

"Before I open this baby," Jocelyn says, pulling the foil from the top of the champagne bottle, "Lacey, you're on music patrol. Put on some fun Christmas music."

How appropriate. Lacey plays "All I Want For Christmas Is You" from Mariah Carey. One of my all-time favorites. Jocelyn wiggles the cork carefully. A second later, it pops, and we twitch from the sound. She fills our glasses, then turns toward me.

"No wedding dresses today, but who knows?" She grins mischievously at me. "Right now, we're going to find you a classy dress perfect for a dinner party at home. Not too fancy but enough to show that it's a special occasion."

Okay. My usual attire at business dinners is black—whether a suit or a dress. Always very business and basic. AKA boring. It'll be fun to finally dress up for real.

Jocelyn pours the popping, golden liquid in the glasses, careful not to overflow. "Let's make a toast to next Saturday and hope that everything runs smoothly. We're all waiting to see Drew's new collection. It's so nerve-racking that he won't show anybody anything. But we trust him."

"Hey, Chatty Cathy, stop talking so I can take a sip," Lacey interrupts.

We lift our glasses. "To Saturday," we say in unison.

Lacey sighs and closes her eyes. "Delicious. I needed that."

Jocelyn pulls me off the couch and looks me up and down. "You have a gorgeous hourglass figure. So let me guess. Your dress size is an eight or ten. But you're from Europe. That means between thirty-eight and forty."

"Not bad. You're right. Depending on the designer, it fluctuates. Either my boobs or ass—usually one or the other is too big. It's so annoying. It's not easy for me to find a dress that fits perfectly and doesn't need any alterations."

"Don't you worry about that. As I said, I can sew. Next on the list, color. I suggest we start with different shades of blue to match your beautiful eyes." She glances at Lacey, who's enjoying another glass of champagne. "Chime in whenever you want, you big lush," she jokes.

"Fully agree. I already have my eye on one, but let's see if I'm correct. If I am, it proves I've learned a lot from you, Jocelyn."

Jocelyn searches through the blue dresses, pulls out a few, and hangs them outside the dressing room.

"Can I ask you both a question?" I hesitate. "Are Christian and Drew not getting along? I know there's some tension, and Christian doesn't seem thrilled with me. But I could be wrong—we've only just met. I don't want to cause any problems by attending this party."

Jocelyn huffs. "First, let me apologize for Christian. He's always overly stressed at the end of the year. He's an investor, and he has more than Devlin Designs to worry about. But he's afraid that you're a distraction and that Drew won't follow through with the project on time."

"That's true," Lacey adds. "But don't take anything he says personally. Christian's been working on this a long time. He'll be crushed if this deal falls through."

"Well, if there's that much pressure flying around, maybe I really shouldn't be there."

Lacey stands up and approaches me. "No, Sophia. Drew wants you there. He wouldn't have asked you if he thought it'd cause a problem. He's got a big crush on you."

"I think it's more than a crush," Jocelyn says. I look over, and she's making heart figures with her hands.

My cheeks burn instantly. "I have a crush too," I say shyly. "Maybe more than a crush."

Lacey claps. "I knew it! So even the more reason to make you beautiful for next weekend."

She walks back to the table, picks up her glass, and resumes her position on the couch.

Jocelyn opens the curtain to the dressing room, then points to me. "You. In there, now. We've got work to do. Lacey's going to hang out on the couch drinking and will be the judge when you come out with the dresses on."

"You know it. I'll try to leave you some." Lacey lifts her glass and takes another long sip. "Now move it."

I glance from one to the other. "I love you both. Thank you for letting me feel like a princess for a day."

I'm not sure I'll feel like one on Saturday.

11

DREW

My nerves are at an all-time high. Tonight had better go as I've planned. I pull on my collar and loosen my awful tie as I pace back and forth in the spare bedroom next to Christian's office. I hate wearing suits. Christian loves it. It's amazing how different we are. He's not happy that I invited Sophia because he still thinks she's a bad influence, but I've ignored him.

I stroll over to the dresser where several black jewelry boxes sit. One is for Sophia now, and the others are for later. When Lacey told me what they had planned for Sophia with regards to dress shopping, I made two little requests and swore Lacey to secrecy. I asked that the dress be some shade of dark blue and have a V neck. I can't wait to see what they've chosen.

There's a light knock on the door. "She's ready. Go upstairs," Lacey announces.

I glance in the mirror one more time and straighten my tie.

"Wait." Lacey stops me after I walk out the door and wraps me in her arms. "Good luck tonight. Thanks for trusting me to help you out. She's a keeper."

I squeeze her back. "Did I ever tell you you're the best sister?"

She squints her eyes. "I'm your only sister."

I chuckle. "Yeah, but seriously, you're the best." She beams and walks away.

I pick up the jewelry box meant for Sophia and head upstairs. Once I approach the door and knock, my heart begins to pound in my ears. It feels like prom night.

"Come in."

I take a deep breath and open the door, hiding the box behind me. All wind is sucked out of my lungs. She's wearing a navy-blue, long-sleeved, wide V-necked satin dress. The hemline rests above her knees. Her hair is up with loose strands falling to the sides.

She pats down her dress. I approach her and take her hand. "Sophia, I've thought you were beautiful every time I've seen you, but tonight I have no words. Beautiful doesn't come close to how you look."

Her angelic face lights up the entire room. "You look quite handsome yourself, for someone who hates to wear suits. It'll be hard to keep my eyes off you." She wiggles my tie.

"But I have to say—"

Her eyebrows crinkle together, and she looks down at her dress. "But what?"

"One thing is missing." I pull the box from behind me and open it.

Her shaky hand covers her mouth, then her glistening eyes lock with mine. "Oh, Drew. It's the necklace I loved the first time I met you."

"I want you to wear it. Please. It's perfect for your dress. It's perfect for you."

Without touching it, she inspects the necklace. I pull it out, then place the box on the table. "Turn around, please. Like you did when you blew into my store and changed my life." She looks over her shoulder and, by impulse, I devour her mouth with mine. I pull away slowly.

"That should get me through half the night. We'll have to see about the second half. I've missed you these past days."

She fans herself, wipes the corner of her mouth and then mine. "I'm glad I'm only wearing lip gloss. We'd both look like clowns if I had worn lipstick."

"Me too. But seriously now. The guests will be here soon." I close the clasp. "There. Look in the mirror."

She twirls around. "It looks beautiful with this dress."

I offer my arm and she wraps hers around it. "Let's get this over with because, when it's done, I'm taking you home and showing you what I really wish we were doing tonight."

"Thank you for everything. I don't think you need it, but good luck."

I kiss her forehead. "Thanks. But I'm not sure it'll be that easy."

~

The doorbell jingles, and my heart starts to pound. I don't know why I'm so nervous. I've already met Alfred, though I haven't met his wife. Maybe it's because Christian has asked me so many questions today. After much deliberation, we've decided to enjoy dinner and then, right before dessert, I'll present the new collection. He still has no idea how I plan to do it.

Christian answers the door as I stand behind him. The women are waiting in the living room.

"Good evening, Alfred. Merry Christmas. It's nice to see you again. Welcome to my home," Christian says. They shake hands.

"Good evening. Let me introduce you to my wife, Britta. Her English is not that good, so I might need to translate throughout the evening."

Christian shakes her hand.

I approach them and introduce myself to his wife as well. I can't help my grin as I say, "My girlfriend is here, and she's from Germany too. I think we're in good hands tonight."

"Wonderful," Alfred responds.

We take their coats and usher them into the living room. Christian introduces Jocelyn and Lacey.

I embrace Sophia's hand with mine and whisper to her that Alfred's wife doesn't speak English well. She squeezes my hand in understanding.

"These are the Waldeckers from Juwelier Belser. Alfred and Britta, my girlfriend, Sophia."

Sophia rattles off something in German, then they shake hands warmly.

"Please, call us Alfred and Britta. I hear you're from Germany."

"Munich, actually. I know your store. You have beautiful jewelry. I can see why you'd be interested in Drew's designs." She rubs my back.

She turns to Britta and translates to her what she said. Britta's face lights up, and they talk for a few moments.

"Jocelyn, Britta says you have a lovely home. She adores American architecture and the Christmas decorations."

"Thank you so much."

And just like that, the evening is off to a smooth start. Drinks flow and conversation is at a friendly level. We've all agreed to save business for after the main course. Sophia continues to translate for Britta when the women are talking.

She helps add life to the conversations with Alfred too. They talk about where they live and how they like Munich. He asks about her job and why she's living here for a while. German and English mix together. I'm so proud of her. Her intelligence shines through. Her relaxed demeanor keeps the conversations flowing, and even Christian seems impressed. Finally.

I find her hand under the table and caress the top with my thumb. Everyone else is distracted, enjoying the first course. She turns to me and I whisper, "You're the most amazing woman. Thanks for being here with me."

"My pleasure. I'm enjoying myself. They are really nice people."

"Sophia," Britta says. She says something in German, and Sophia responds, touching the sapphire pendant.

She lifts it and turns toward me again. "Britta just complimented this necklace. I explained to her it's one of yours."

Britta looks at me. "Beautiful."

"I told her it's my favorite from you."

Britta taps Alfred's arm and points to the necklace and says something to him. He glances at it, nods, and responds to her.

Sophia leans to me and whispers, "She's telling him how much she loves this necklace and is looking forward to seeing the new collection."

"I brought some other jewelry from the store, in addition to the new ones I'll present them. He's seen a lot already, but it sounds like his wife will be interested in them."

"The main dish is ready," Jocelyn announces. "I hope you're hungry."

We finish dinner and Jocelyn and Lacey clear the table. Christian asks if we want to retire to the living room and finally talk business.

I stand to follow them out, then clear my throat.

"I'll be with you in a moment," I inform them. Christian's eyes warn me that this had better work. He hasn't told them he hasn't seen the collection yet.

"Sophia. Will you come with me, please? I need your help with something." She follows me to the hallway.

"Is everything all right?" she asks.

Christian excuses himself and walks up behind us. "What are you doing? Why do you need Sophia's help?" Nasty Christian is back because it's time to talk business. We're going to have a long talk after this meeting. I'm tired of the way he treats her like she's not there or unwanted.

"Don't start," I warn him. "We'll be back in a moment."

His jawline twitches, but Jocelyn calls him from the living room and he walks away.

I lead Sophia past Christian's office to the spare bedroom. Once I close the door, I embrace her. "Thank you. I can't say it enough. You were brilliant in there. I'm so impressed."

Her face softens and turns a sweet shade of pink. "You're welcome. Why shouldn't I contribute when I have the experience? I think the evening is going really well. Where are you hiding the new collection?"

I walk over to the dresser where the other jewelry boxes are, and she follows.

Her face lights up. "Oh my gosh. Can I see them?"

I chuckle. "You're so cute when you get excited. Can you take off the necklace, please?"

"Umm. Okay." She removes it and hands it to me. I place it on top of the dresser because I forgot the box upstairs.

Here goes nothing. I hand her one of the other boxes. "Go ahead."

She takes it in her hands and opens it carefully. Her mouth drops open. "Drew! I'm absolutely speechless. It's stunning. I love it more than any design I've seen from you."

We move near a lamp on the dresser. "The intricate detail of this snowflake is so delicate, and the diamonds make it glisten like when the sun shines on a fresh bed of snow. The striking deep-blue sapphire accents make it even more breathtaking. The size of the pendant is perfect—at least to me. It's not overpowering."

"I'm glad you like it, because I want you to wear it."

"Me? Now?" She shakes her head. "I can't do that."

"Please. I've envisioned this night since I met you. You inspired this design. If anyone should wear it, it should be you. Your dress is perfect to show it off. It's so much better than presenting it in a box. Please wear it."

Her tense eyebrows relax and the sides of her sexy mouth rise. "When you put it like that, I'd love to."

I raise my finger. "One more thing—well, two. I've also made matching earrings and a bracelet."

"Should I wear those too?"

"Of course." I remove them from their boxes, and hand her the earrings first.

Knock, knock. "Drew, Christian's starting to twitch. Hurry up," Lacey whispers through the door.

"We're coming," I say.

Sophia puts the earrings on, then I fasten the bracelet on her wrist. "Thank you for trusting me with these. It means the world to me." She kisses me sweetly. "Let's get this show on the road."

Each piece fits perfectly on her. We both stare at her in the mirror. Her eyes glisten. "I feel like a princess."

I press my lips to her temple. "No. You're my queen. Now let's go."

A few seconds later, I lead Sophia into the living room. Her hand is cold, so I know she's nervous. "Everyone." The group turns toward us. "I'd like to introduce to you my new collection. I thought it would be nicer to see it on someone than show it in a box."

The women gasp. Britta rubs Alfred's arm and whispers something. Her wide eyes and zealous smile show me she likes it. Jocelyn and Lacey babble behind us. Christian stands next to me.

"Great job. I'm sorry I doubted you, Drew. It's the best you've ever done." Christian holds out his hand to shake mine. I take it.

"Thanks. That means a lot."

Alfred looks at Sophia. "May I?" He points to the necklace.

"Yes, of course."

Alfred and Britta walk up to her and observe the pieces but don't touch them. Britta stares at the bracelet, and Sophia extends her arm so she can look at it.

"What's the name of this collection?"

I gaze at Sophia. "It's called *Sophia* because she's my inspiration." Her eyes flash with surprise, then soften.

There's silence in the room for a brief moment, and then Lacey speaks up. "That's so romantic. I love it, Drew."

Britta nods too, and Alfred smiles. I release the breath that I didn't know I was holding. A smile is a good thing.

"Can you explain this collection? Is it one of a kind?"

"There's no snowflake exactly alike. My idea is that the pieces in the collection would be unique snowflakes with different gems. They don't have to include sapphires. The customer can choose. I haven't made a ring yet, but that will be included in the set. I can also make the pendants larger or smaller. These are the details we can discuss later. I have several designs on my laptop that I can show you if you are interested."

Alfred crosses his arms and rests his chin on his hand. "I'm definitely interested. May I examine the pieces?" He smiles at Sophia. "I'm sorry. I have a feeling you don't want to let them go. They look stunning on you."

He retrieves his case from the hallway and pulls

out some tools. I remove the jewels from Sophia and hand them over. One by one, he examines the pieces thoroughly and asks several questions for which I have extensive answers.

"Exquisite. You do exceptional work."

"Thank you, sir."

Several minutes of discussion ensue, then Alfred extends his hand to me. "Congratulations, Drew, Christian. I think we have a deal."

After Alfred and Britta drive away in a taxi, we all scream in delight.

"I'm so proud of you. You deserve this," Sophia says, and she kisses me. "But if you'll excuse me, I need to go to the bathroom."

Christian pats me on the back. "Can I talk to you in my office for a second?"

"Sure." I remove the tie that has felt like a noose all night.

"Jocelyn, maybe another bottle of champagne is needed," Christian says. "We should celebrate." Finally he's happy.

We walk into his pristine office, and I close the door part way. "What's up?"

He puts his hands on my shoulders and a sly smile grows on his face, transfixing him into the Joker. "I can't believe I questioned you. You set this up impeccably." His fingers dig into my shoulders as he shakes me. "Sophia was a perfect decoy."

I shrug him off me. "What the hell are you talking about?"

He punches the air in excitement. I've never seen him like this. "Come on. It's so obvious now."

"What is? I'm completely lost."

He walks over to the humidor on the wall and removes a Cuban cigar. He drags it under his nose and sniffs it. "All the secrecy. With Sophia's background, it's awesome that you took advantage of her skills. You set it up like she's your girlfriend and in love, so it looks even more convincing. Little did they know, you've only known each other for a couple of days. His wife probably loved it that you named the collection after Sophia. Just brilliant."

"It wasn't like that," I interject.

He cackles, then takes a lighter off the top of the humidor. "You asked Jocelyn and Lacey to help her pick out the perfect dress. And then you, showing her the diamond and sapphire the other night. I couldn't have planned it better myself. You've learned well."

He struts out of the office, then yells over his shoulder, "Let's go outside for a smoke."

"Christian, we need to talk. *Now*. You have it all wrong."

"Then come outside with me. We deserve a smoke."

Lacey rushes up to me. "What happened? Sophia just ran upstairs and wouldn't tell me what's wrong."

I'll deal with Christian later.

"Is she sick?"

"I don't think so. She looked really pissed. Go after her." She points to the stairs.

"Don't bother," Sophia snaps as she begins to descend the stairs. "I don't want you anywhere near me." Her blue eyes are like ice. No reflection of love anymore. She's taken the dress off and is back in her own clothes.

Jocelyn runs out from the kitchen, and Christian turns around to see what's going on.

Sophia storms to the closet and yanks her coat off the hanger. I carefully approach her.

"What's the matter? Why are you so angry?"

She shoves her arm through one side of the coat and then the other. "Next time you have a little meeting with Christian in his precious office, close the damn door. I heard what he said."

Oh shit.

"Christian, what did you do?" Jocelyn's usual happy mood now oozes with anger.

"You used me this entire time? Your little *decoy*, as Christian called me? How could you? I can't believe I was so stupid to have trusted someone I hardly knew. I should blame myself."

"Sophia, it wasn't like that at all," Lacey expresses.

"Oh, *really*? Is it true about the dress? Did Drew ask you to find me the perfect dress?" She glares at Lacey and then Jocelyn.

Lacey steps forward with her hands up at her sides. "Yes, but it's not what you think. This is all a misunderstanding."

"How convenient that the dress was blue and V cut. Perfect for displaying a sapphire necklace. You're all a bunch of great actors, aren't you? I fell for it, and so did the Waldeckers. You deserve Oscars."

"Sophia, let's go somewhere to talk. Christian didn't give me the chance to defend myself in there. He's got everything wrong. *Everything.*"

"What do you mean?" Christian comes closer. Jocelyn grabs his elbow and tells him to be quiet.

"Christian, you've done enough damage, so I suggest you stay right there and keep your fucking mouth shut," I demand.

"Who do you think you're talking to?"

"An asshole who looks like my brother."

Jocelyn gives me a dirty look, but I don't care.

"Don't leave, Sophia. We need to talk. I can clear up this mess."

"I'm not going anywhere with you. I'm walking out this door, and you're never going to see me again." She storms out of the house.

Jocelyn and Lacey yell her name. I run out the door after her.

"Please, stop. Let me explain." The cold air smacks me in the face. Or was it her hand?

"Why should I listen to you? Give me one reason."

"Because I love you, damn it." I kick a crusted pile of snow beside the walk. "This is not how I wanted to tell you."

Clouds plume from her mouth as she snickers. "You don't love me. You only love your business. Just like your pitiful brother. It makes me sick that I gave you my heart. I think about the night we spent together during the storm, and I feel repulsed." That hurt.

"Sophia." I rub my hands over my face. "This is fucking nuts. Christian came up with all that nonsense back there. You can't have heard everything because I tried to tell him he was wrong. He didn't give me the chance to say it, but he's full of shit. He's in his own little world right now. Please believe me. Everything I did was because I love you. Any chance I had to make you smile and be happy, I did it. I wanted you here tonight because I wanted you by my side. Nothing else. Yes, it helped that you spoke German and were able to facilitate our business discussions, but that was not why I asked you to be here."

She shakes her head and walks backward. "I can't. You may not wear suits, but you act like every other suit I've ever worked with. And Christian is worse. Only out for the money; never thinking about how your actions affect the people around you. I pity you people."

"How could you trust Christian's word over mine? I love you. I never thought I would fall so quickly for a woman like I did for you. Don't walk away from us." I'm groveling.

"There is no us. There never was. It was all an illusion." Her voice cracks, and her eyes shimmer with tears. "Don't follow me, don't call me, and don't come to my apartment. I'm done. Thanks for the Christmas I'll never forget and for breaking my heart. There's always a first for everything." Sarcasm and disdain exude from her voice. She turns and strides down the street, motioning for a taxi nearby.

I stand frozen to the ground, watching the woman I love drive away from me.

The front door opens, and the girls stand in the doorway. I run up the stairs and storm into the house. "Christian," I yell. Lacey and Jocelyn scurry behind me.

He faces the fireplace and leans against the mantle with one hand.

"You ruined everything," I shout. "Everything." My chest heaves from the anger that's building up.

He shrugs. "We got the deal. That's all that matters."

"Christian, how dare you?" Jocelyn glowers. "Look at me!"

He turns slowly toward us; his face lacks any sign of emotion. Jocelyn stands tall and points her finger at him. "I don't know what's going on with you, but you've been a complete jackass these last couple of months. And that's me being nice right now. I've tried to be patient, but I'm at my limit after tonight. The only thing you care about is money and yourself. Everything is about making a deal."

With crossed arms, he says to me, "You can't possibly tell me you love Sophia. You hardly know her, and you haven't even talked about her with me."

"Why don't you think about that for a second? Maybe it's because you never ask. You just demand. You treat your clients better than your own family."

"If you opened your eyes, you would've seen how he feels about her," Lacey points out. "I've known about everything since he met Sophia. Never once was his intention business. Yes, he asked me to help her pick out a dress so she'd feel special. He wanted to make her happy and to show how she inspired him. And now you've ruined everything."

"You've neglected everyone in your family for a long time now," I continue. "When's the last time you spent any real time with Coral or Jocelyn?"

He pounces toward me. "Don't you dare talk about my relationship with my family."

"Why not? Are you afraid of the truth? You neglect them."

Jocelyn stands in front of Christian in warning. "Drew. Stop."

I raise my hand. "No, Jocelyn. He needs to hear it." I poke my finger toward his chest. When I'm with you, you only talk about business. You never ask how I'm doing. It's the same with Lacey. When's the last time you've had a conversation with her about anything? She only comes over here to hang out with Jocelyn and Coral, not you. And that's because you have your head so far up your ass, you don't even know she's here. But now, you've gone too far."

"What is that supposed to mean?" he retorts.

"If I lose Sophia, this deal's off. I don't want to work with someone who only cares about himself. Sophia means more to me than anything I own. I don't care if I lose the store or anything else."

12

SOPHIA

"After what you told me about him, I can't imagine he'd do that to you. You always got a bad vibe from Christian, so why do you trust his word over Drew's?"

"He didn't deny it when they were in Christian's office, Tessa." *Sniff.* I didn't cry in front of Drew. I wouldn't give him the satisfaction. But once I got in the taxi, I cried all the way home.

"But you said you ran off before the conversation was over."

I plunge backward onto my bed and stare at the ceiling. My room seemed like the better place to talk to Tessa on the phone. I don't want to see the Christmas tree. "I know. But when I go over the events since I met him, it adds up to what Christian said. Everything he did could've been for business. The whole thing could've been an act."

"When you first met him, you were head over heels, and he didn't know about your background. He seemed just as attracted to you. And Lacey and Jocelyn don't sound like they have a mean bone in their bodies."

My heart aches more than it ever has. I wish I could remove it and hide it somewhere so it can't be broken again.

"How did you feel when he said he loved you?"

"My heart raced with love for him… and then I remembered why I was mad."

"You love him, Sophia. Now, I realize time doesn't make a difference. When you know, you know. And I'm positive you know how you feel."

"My mind is all over the place. I can't do anything right now until the dust settles. Why does it have to be Christmas Eve tomorrow?"

"I wish I could've visited you. I hate that you'll be all alone on Christmas. We should be out at a bar right now."

I giggle. "I'm not sure getting drunk would make me feel any better. But it's a nice thought. I can lay in bed all day, since it's Sunday."

"Listen, I need to go. I wish you luck. That's all I can do. Call me tonight."

"Okay. Love you."

"Love you too."

I disconnect and let the phone fall from my hand onto the bed. I want to believe Drew, but it was almost scary how conniving Christian was… or is. Tessa's right, though. I didn't stay long enough to hear Drew's response.

Without changing into my pajamas, I wrap myself

up in my blanket like a cocoon. A lone tear escapes my eye and falls onto my pillow. Within seconds I'm asleep.

The nonstop ringing of my doorbell snaps me out of oblivion. A noise I used to love is now like fingernails on a chalkboard. It takes me a minute to orient myself. I look at the clock. I feel like I've only been sleeping for a few minutes, but the clock says something else. I've slept ten hours!

The bell rings again. I cover my ears. It's either Drew or Lacey. I ignore it and wander to the bathroom. It rings again. And then again. *What the hell?* I flush the toilet. It rings again. Okay, now I'm pissed.

I stomp over to the door and hit the intercom button. "What do you want? I told you not to contact me or come here."

"It's Christian."

I purse my lips and squeeze my eyes shut.

"Why the hell would I want to see you?"

"Because I was wrong. Please, hear me out, and I'll leave you alone."

"Wait outside. I'll be out in a few minutes. This better be worth my while." I don't want him in my apartment. I'll let him freeze out there to torture him a little longer. He deserves it.

Ten minutes pass before I finally walk out the front entrance. Christian leans against the side of the building. He looks like he hasn't slept in weeks. His ears and cheeks are bright red. I'm surprised icicles aren't forming off his earlobes. He pushes off the wall and approaches me.

"Thank you for coming out," he says, lacking his normal confidence.

"Did he send you?"

"No. Lacey wanted to come but I convinced her to let me instead. I need to make things right because it's all my fault. She told me where you live."

I might be mad at her too, but I can't help to want to smile. It's so like her.

"I knew you wouldn't answer the door right away, so I kept ringing, praying you'd be home and answer."

"So? I'm here. Let's get this over with." The arctic air spikes my anger. I'm starting to hate New York in winter, but I know it's my foul mood talking. I wrap my arms tightly around my waist.

"I'm sorry for what happened last night. Hell broke loose when you left. All three of them told me off and made me realize what an asshole I've become. I've forgotten what's important in my life. I'm nothing without my family. Money is nice, but it's not worth losing the ones I love."

I look up at the sky and then back at him. "Seriously? You expect me to believe that you've figured all this out in so little time?"

"I had a heart-to-heart with Drew. Everything you heard me say was my asshole self talking. I can't explain it. Maybe I would've done what I accused Drew of doing, I don't know. But Drew wouldn't hurt anyone deliberately. Yes, I found it ridiculous that he said he loved you after you've known each other for, what, two weeks? Three? But that makes me a hypocrite, because I told Jocelyn on our first date that I was going to marry her one day."

"So what's your point, Christian?"

"I wanted to let you know that I was wrong about everything. Drew loves you. You're a good influence on him, even if I did think you were a bad distraction. The collection he designed was the best he's ever done, and I know now that it was because of you. He deserves to be happy, and he's far from it right now. I hate that I'm the reason why. So I have to fix it… somehow."

"And that would be how?" Now he has me curious.

"I'm here to make things right. He has one wish. Tomorrow night, Christmas Eve, he wishes you'd meet him at the Rockefeller Christmas tree at eleven, where you kissed the first time."

"And if I don't?"

"He'll leave you alone. But I have a feeling he couldn't leave you alone for long. But since it's Christmas, miracles can happen."

"Yeah, well… thank you for coming and apologizing. I need time to think about everything."

"Answer this. Do you love him?"

I glance at the ground and skim my foot over the ice. *Just say it, Sophia.* I look at him. "Yes."

He grins. "Then I hope you find it in your heart to meet him tomorrow night. He'll be waiting. Remember, hate me. I'm the asshole, not him."

He turns away and walks down the street.

13

SOPHIA

It's amazing how busy it is here at this time on Christmas Eve. I didn't think there would still be so many people out this late at night. Don't they have families to visit? I zigzag between bustling bodies, sometimes banging into them with my shoulder.

The angels glow ahead, blowing their horns, announcing that I've arrived. Flurries fly around and land on my heavy coat. I'm colder than usual because of my nerves. This could be a total waste of my time. What if he's changed his mind and doesn't show up?

But he asked me to come here.

My phone says it's ten fifty-five. I'm standing where we first kissed. My feet are frozen, but I won't move from this spot. I keep searching the crowd for Drew's face, but I don't see him. After fifteen minutes, my hopes plummet. He's not coming. Why? Even after what Christian said? I thought this place was magical. What a joke. *I'm so naïve.*

I've lost the only man I've ever loved, and it's

because I jumped to conclusions. *Stay strong and do not cry*. I drop my head in defeat and turn to leave, and then I hear my name. I draw a sharp breath. It was faint, but I know his voice. I look left and right, then I twirl around, searching for him. Praying that he's really here.

"Sophia," he yells.

He's here! I see him in the distance, waving his hand high in the middle of the crowd. My frozen heart begins to defrost.

I push through the crowd to reach him. He's so close.

As if a stronger force was watching, the crowd parts, and it's only him and me. Fluffy clouds of cold air pour from our mouths.

A smile grows on his anxious face, telling me that everything will be okay. He opens his arms, and I jump into them. I shower him with kisses and let the tears fall.

"I didn't think you were coming. I thought I ruined everything and lost you."

He holds my face in his hands. "I'm sorry that everything got so screwed up. You will never lose me. I meant what I said. I love you."

"I love you too," I cry. "I was afraid to admit it because I was scared. I'm not scared anymore."

"Sophia, when I met you, I wasn't supposed to be in the front of the store. But when I saw you, it was like fate sent you there only for me. You were looking at the necklace you liked in the case, and I glanced at your hand and imagined a diamond ring on your finger. One made and given to you by me." He takes my mitten off my left hand and kisses my ring finger.

"Not now, but I promise, one day, I will marry you. I want to wake up every day to your brilliant smile. And I promise to do everything I can to always make you happy."

"Does this mean I won't be moving back to Germany in six months?" I tease.

"Don't even think about it," he smirks. He captures my lips with his. We melt into each other, savoring this moment.

"I've missed your sweet lips and your gentle touch. In such a short time you've become a part of me. I'm so lucky." I brush my lips against his.

"You know—" He kisses me back. "Someone said this place is magical at Christmas time and that dreams come true here. Sophia, you're my dream come true."

"And you're mine. Kiss me again."

"I plan to. For the rest of our lives."

The End

Check out Lacey's story in Passions and Peonies!

ALSO BY KRISTINA BECK

Collide Series

Lives Collide

Dreams Collide

Souls Collide

Collide Series Box Set

Four Seasons Series

Snowflakes and Sapphires - Winter

Passions and Peonies - Spring

Colors and Curves - Summer

Maple Trees and Maybes - Autumn

Standalone Novels

Into Thin Air

Love Ever After Anthology

ACKNOWLEDGMENTS

After I released my last book, I wanted to take a break for a couple of months. I had an idea for a new book but it wasn't something I wanted to write at the time. Then a Christmas story popped into my head and I couldn't ignore it. I only had a couple of months to write it if I wanted to release it before Christmas. That's how Snowflakes and Sapphires came to be. I needed something fun and uplifting.

But then, another idea sprouted for a new series because of this book, called The Four Seasons Novella Series. One of my favorite '80s movie is called *The Four Seasons*. The movie was broken up into each season. My series will do the same. Each book will represent another season and another couple. Snowflakes and Sapphires represents winter. The next book will come out in the spring.

Beta readers are always important for the publishing process. Thank you Ilona and Jamie for your last minute help and great feedback. I value your input and friendship! I hope we can work together again.

The editing process is always exhausting. Rachel Overton of Wordscapes, thank you for fitting me into your schedule with little notice. You drive me nuts with your pickiness but it always makes my books even better. You don't only edit well, you teach well. I've learned so much since I've started. Thank you for your time and patience.

Helen Pryke, thank you for squeezing me into your tight schedule. I know how busy the end of the year can be. Thanks for always letting me vent to you when I'm having a bad day. I know I can always count on you!

Thank you, Jody Kaye, for designing this gorgeous book cover. Your support, expertise, and friendship mean the world to me. I look forward to working with you again.

Rik Hall from Wild Seas Formatting, it's always a pleasure working with you. You make this step of the process so easy. Thank you!!!

To my husband, you begged me to take a break but you knew that I wouldn't. When I have an idea, I have to go with it. I love you and am truly blessed to have your support and love every day. My kids are my biggest fans and advertisers. They always tell random people that I'm an author. It's so embarrassing but it warms my heart that they are so proud of me.

And to all of my readers, thank you for the great

book reviews and sweet messages you send me. Your support and patience pushes me to write the next book even when I'm full of doubt. I hope you enjoy this new series. I can't wait to write the rest of the books.

ABOUT THE AUTHOR

Kristina Beck was born and raised in New Jersey, USA, and lived there for thirty years. She later moved to Germany and lives there with her German husband and three children. She is an avid reader of many genres, but romance always takes precedence. She loves coffee, dark chocolate, power naps, and eighties movies. Her hobbies include writing, reading, fitness, and forever trying to improve her German-language skills.

To receive updates on her new releases, sales, and book signings, signup for her newsletter on her website or follow her on social media.

www.kristinabeck.com

facebook.com/krissybeck73
instagram.com/krissybeck96
amazon.com/author/kristinabeck
bookbub.com/authors/kristina-beck
goodreads.com/kristina_beck

Printed in Great Britain
by Amazon

61713522R00087